PRAISE FOR
ASTROTWINS—PROJECT BLASTOFF

. . . .

"The information imparted is staged just right. Intriguing subject matter and rock-solid pacing combine for a nifty adventure—one that may well spark a new generation of astronauts."—*Kirkus Reviews*

"From bickering twins to space-race history to a secret rocket-fuel formula, this chapter book offers an entertaining mixture of reality, historical fiction, science, and fun."—*Booklist*

"The characters are likable, the dialogue is enlightening as well as snappy, and the adventure is grand; a fine purchase for middle grade collections."—*School Library Journal*

"[R]ealistic sibling and peer relationships, illuminating science, and some streamlined aeronautical history keep the story grounded—in a good way."—*Publishers Weekly*

Also by Mark Kelly
Astrotwins—Project Rescue

MARK KELLY

WITH MARTHA FREEMAN

ASTROTWINS

PROJECT BLASTOFF

A PAULA
WISEMAN BOOK
SIMON & SCHUSTER BOOKS
FOR YOUNG READERS
NEW YORK   LONDON   TORONTO
SYDNEY   NEW DELHI

SIMON & SCHUSTER BOOKS FOR YOUNG READERS
An imprint of Simon & Schuster Children's Publishing Division
1230 Avenue of the Americas, New York, New York 10020

This book is a work of fiction. Any references to historical events, real people, or real places are used fictitiously. Other names, characters, places, and events are products of the author's imagination, and any resemblance to actual events or places or persons, living or dead, is entirely coincidental.

For information about special discounts for bulk purchases, please contact Simon & Schuster Special Sales at 1-866-506-1949 or business@simonandschuster.com.
The Simon & Schuster Speakers Bureau can bring authors to your live event. For more information or to book an event, contact the Simon & Schuster Speakers Bureau at 1-866-248-3049 or visit our website at www.simonspeakers.com.
Also available in a Simon & Schuster Books for Young Readers hardcover edition
Book design by Chloë Foglia
The text for this book was set in Minister Std.
Manufactured in the United States of America
0216 OFF
First Simon & Schuster Books for Young Readers paperback edition March 2016
2 4 6 8 10 9 7 5 3 1
The Library of Congress has cataloged the hardcover edition as follows:
Kelly, Mark E.
Astrotwins—project blastoff / Mark Kelly with Martha Freeman.
pages cm—(Astrotwins)
"A Paula Wiseman Book."
Summary: "Twins Mark and Scott Kelly decide to build a rocket over the summer when their constant bickering starts to annoy their grandfather in this middle-grade novel based on the NASA astronauts' real childhoods"—Provided by publisher. Includes facts about NASA and the space program.
ISBN 978-1-4814-1545-3 (hc)
1. Kelly, Mark E.—Childhood and youth—Juvenile fiction. 2. Kelly, Scott, 1964– —Childhood and youth—Juvenile fiction. [1. Kelly, Mark E.—Childhood and youth—Fiction. 2. Kelly, Scott, 1964– —Childhood and youth—Fiction.
3. Brothers—Fiction. 4. Twins—Fiction. 5. Rockets (Aeronautics)—Fiction.
6. Grandfathers—Fiction.] I. Freeman, Martha, 1956—II. Title. III.
Title: Project blastoff.
PZ7.K296395Ast 2014
[Fic]—dc23
2014012400
ISBN 978-1-4814-1546-0 (pbk)
ISBN 978-1-4814-1547-7 (eBook)

To my brother, Scott, who is spending one year off the planet to advance our understanding of how humans can live in space for extended periods of time.

—M. K.

CHAPTER 1

JULY 18, 1975

This time the twins were determined. Nothing would go wrong.

Scott had stationed Major Nelson, the family's big, brown, friendly mutt, at the back door to bark if Mom came home early.

Mark had laid newspapers on Dad's basement workbench.

They had assembled their tools.

And they were absolutely going to follow the advice Grandpa Joe gave them for anytime you took something apart: Lay the parts down in order so when you put the pieces back together, you can simply reverse the process.

Easy!

"It's like Grandpa Joe always says: Learn from your mistakes," Mark said.

"Yeah, and since we've made so many, we ought to be geniuses by now," Scott agreed.

Mark laughed. "Okay, so go ahead. I'll keep everything organized."

With a screwdriver made for repairing eyeglasses, Scott removed two screws, which Mark placed in the top left corner of the newspaper.

Then—the best part—Scott removed the plastic backplate and the boys got their first look inside Dad's calculator.

"Cool!" they chorused.

Exposed, the insides resembled staples, pushpins, and grains of rice, all of them tiny and arrayed around a white plastic rectangle. The biggest piece was the battery, which was easy to recognize and easy to remove. After that, there were six more screws.

Mark duly put each in its place on the newspaper.

"Should we take out the CPU?" Scott asked.

Mark knew *CPU* stood for "central processing unit," that it was made of a material called silicon, and that it was the brains of the calculator. What he didn't know was which piece it was, but no way was he going to admit that to his brother. "Sure," he said.

Scott used the tip of the screwdriver to pry up the white plastic rectangle, and out it popped.

"Are you sure you can plug that back in there?" Mark asked.

"You mean, am I sure *we* can plug it back in there?" Scott said. "Yeah, of course. I think. And these are transistors, right?" He indicated black spheres that looked like beads.

Mark nodded. "I guess, but they sure look different from the ones in the TV." Years ago, the boys had watched fascinated as the TV repairman worked on their old black-and-white set. After that, they decided to see what was inside other machines, like the clock radio, the sewing machine, and the lawn mower.

Usually, they got in trouble, but it was worth it.

Scott had just lifted up the calculator to examine the underside of the display when Major Nelson's excited barking made him jump. "She's home!" he said.

"She's early!" Mark said.

"She won't come down here," Scott said. "Will she?"

"We can't take that chance," Mark said and, hurrying, handed his brother each calculator piece to replace. Upstairs, their mom's heels clicked on the kitchen floor as she put groceries away. Another sound—*thump-thump-thump*—meant Major Nelson was bounding all around her, hoping for a treat.

So focused were the boys on reassembly that they didn't realize the danger till they heard Mom's heels echoing on the wooden basement steps. By now the boys had been in this predicament so often, they knew the countdown.

3 . . . Scott closed his eyes, prepared to accept his fate.

2 . . . Mark made a last-ditch attempt to hide what they'd been doing, in the process yanking the newspaper off the workbench.

1 . . . Mom appeared in the doorway, just in time to see a scattering of tiny calculator parts bouncing every which way on the floor.

Ignition: *"Boys!"* Mom cried. "What in the heck have you done now?"

CHAPTER 2

After the calculator catastrophe, Scott and Mark estimated they'd be grounded for approximately one century, with maybe a decade off for good behavior.

But that wasn't what happened.

Instead, once the initial lecture was over, Mom and Dad took the whole thing surprisingly calmly. And the next day they announced they were packing the boys off to Grandpa Joe's for a week. Grandpa Joe McAvoy was their mom's dad, a widower who lived in a cabin by a lake about an hour's drive north by car, near the New York–New Jersey state line.

"You mean, instead of punishing us, you're rewarding us?" Mark asked.

"That doesn't make any sense," Scott said. "I mean . . . not that it's a bad idea, though."

"It's an excellent idea," said Mark. "And we're really sorry about the calculator."

"We told you that already, right?" Scott said.

"You did," said Mr. Kelly. He wasn't smiling, but he wasn't yelling either. "Your mom and I think the trouble is, you're bored around the house. Grandpa Joe's got plenty of work for you to do."

"Our idea is, you'll be so busy at Grandpa's, you won't have time to get in trouble," Mom concluded. "Get it?"

"Got it," said Mark and Scott.

"Good," said their parents.

The Kelly family lived in a friendly neighborhood in West Orange, New Jersey—only fifteen miles from New York City. The Kellys' two-story house was gray rock with white trim and very well kept because, as their dad put it, there were two healthy boys to serve as slave labor. Since Mr. and Mrs. Kelly both worked long hours at hard jobs, Mark and Scott mowed the lawn, mulched the flower beds, watered, and weeded. But the yard was small. So in summer, there was plenty of time left over for goofing around . . . and getting bored.

Mark and Scott were the only kids in their family. Their parents said two were plenty when they were as rough-and-tumble as the twins. The boys were alike in many ways—good at sports, curious about everything, and fast learners when they wanted to be.

But there were differences, too.

Mark was inclined both to act first and speak first. He liked to tease his brother. There was trouble when he didn't get his way.

Scott was more even-tempered and usually thought before speaking. He also had a good sense of humor about himself, which was kind of a requirement for getting along with his brother.

The next day was Sunday. Mr. Kelly was a police officer who often worked nights, so in the morning he drove the boys north in the family's Ford Country Squire station wagon with wood paneling on the side.

The drive was mostly on the highway. The car had no air-conditioning. The ride was hot and boring, and both boys fell asleep. When they woke up, it was because the car was bump-bumping along the ruts of their grandfather's unpaved driveway.

"Where's Grandpa Joe?" Mark asked a few minutes later. He and Scott had dumped their duffel bags in Twin Territory, which is what they called the second-floor loft where they always slept. The house, as always, was unlocked. Grandpa said that if he wanted to lock his doors, he would have stayed in the city.

"Search me," Mr. Kelly said. "I told him what time we'd be getting here, give or take."

"Hello-o-o!" a voice called from the path leading to the shore of nearby Greenwood Lake. Scott, Mark, and their dad turned, and here came Grandpa, wearing denim overalls with no shirt underneath.

Dad shook his head and laughed. "Ever the snappy dresser, Joseph."

Grandpa tugged at the shoulder straps. "You like the Farmer John look, eh? Well, of course you do! Overalls provide all the ventilation you could want on a hot day, plus you can't beat 'em for comfort. Now, how are my outlaw grandsons?"

Grandpa Joe had served in the merchant marine and later captained a fireboat in New York Harbor. Now, depending on the day of the week, he identified his occupation as either farmer, architect, or mechanic.

He was a farmer because he had a patch of vegetables planted behind the house and two hens whose eggs he could never find.

He was an architect because he had designed and built his house himself—or, more accurately, was working on designing and building it. Not all the rooms had walls, and parts of the roof were just blue tarp.

And he was a mechanic because he had a rusted-out Model A pickup truck up on blocks beside the house and a barn he used as a workshop out back. Brimming with tools, parts, bits, pieces, junk, discards, cobwebs, grease, and gewgaws, the workshop was a source of endless fascination to the twins, in part because they were never allowed to visit without strict supervision.

Grandpa said he was afraid that otherwise they might blow something up.

Neither Dad nor Grandpa was a hugger, so the two shook hands and slapped backs and said, "Great to see you." Then they all went inside and rustled up bread, apples, and peanut butter for lunch. Peanut butter, in Grandpa's opinion, was the perfect food.

They ate at a picnic table under a tree, and then Dad said he had to leave to get to work. "Be good, boys. And do what your grandpa tells you."

"We will, Dad," said Mark.

"We promise," said Scott.

CHAPTER 3

Usually, Mark and Scott loved visiting their grandfather in the summertime, but this time they'd forgotten one thing. Grandpa didn't have a TV!

This wouldn't have mattered so much except that their visit overlapped with the last few days of an important NASA mission, the one where space modules from the U.S.A. and the Soviet Union met in orbit. On Thursday, Scott and Mark had watched the docking of the Apollo and Soyuz spacecraft; then, later, they watched the astronauts and cosmonauts floating through the hatch and shaking hands.

The Russian crew had returned to Earth already, but the three Americans wouldn't splash down till Thursday. TV would cover it live, and Mark and Scott didn't want to miss it.

"I don't see what the trouble is," their grandfather said. "You can read all about it in the newspaper on Friday."

"The newspaper?" Mark couldn't believe he was related to anyone so old-fashioned. "That's nowhere nearly as good as seeing it live on TV!"

Grandpa put his hand to his ear and said, "Hmm. That sound I hear couldn't be whining, could it?"

Mark sighed. "No, sir," he said. "Absolutely not."

Even without television, the week passed quickly. As predicted, Grandpa found plenty for them to do—like washing windows, painting the porch, weeding the garden, and gathering the always elusive eggs. On the rare times that Grandpa didn't have a job for them, there were woods where they could wander and build forts, and a lake where they could row a boat and swim.

Both boys were skillful tree climbers. Mark made a game out of climbing as high as he could. Scott liked to find a fat branch on which to sit and contemplate the world.

Finally it was Friday, the day the boys had been dreading. On Friday, a *girl* had been invited to come over and eat lunch.

"She's going into sixth grade like you are and she's not icky or anything. You'll like her," Grandpa had said.

The boys couldn't believe it. Didn't Grandpa remember being a kid? Didn't he remember how uncool it was to hang out with a girl? How could he assume you'd get along with a total stranger, a female total stranger, just because she happened to be in the same grade as you?

Mark had argued.

Scott had sulked.

But nothing worked, and at lunchtime Jenny O'Malley arrived in a beat-up Ford Falcon with her mom and a homemade blueberry pie. Jenny had wavy brown hair and freckles. She was wearing cutoffs and a blue T-shirt and tennis shoes with no socks.

She looked normal enough.

And the pie was delicious.

Jenny didn't say much while they ate, but her mom talked a lot, and Grandpa laughed at the stuff she said. After lunch, Jenny's mom actually uttered these words: "Now, you kids run along and play for a bit before we have to go home. Don't you want to get to know each other?"

Jenny looked appropriately mortified. Mark thought he would have died if his own mom had ever said anything that dumb.

But Scott got up from the table and said, "Come on," without looking at anyone, and the three of them took off for the shore of the lake.

Mark was more talkative than his brother and—he wasn't proud of this—cared more about what other people thought. So when they got to the lakeshore, it was Mark who said, "Uh, I liked the pie. Did you make it? Or your mom?"

"I did," Jenny said. "My mom doesn't really cook."

"That makes you an engineer, in a way," Mark said. "You took flour, water, butter, and blueberries—then you engineered a pie out of 'em."

Jenny grinned. "That's a good way to think about it."

After that, they skipped stones on the water, and one of Jenny's bounced five times. "Good one," Mark said.

Jenny shrugged. "I get a lot of practice." Then she put her hands in her pockets. "You know, coming here today wasn't my idea. My mom said I had to."

"Yeah?" Scott looked up.

"So that's okay, then," Mark said.

After that, it was easier to talk, and it turned out Jenny was interested in space stuff too. The science teacher at her school—Mr. Drizzle—launched homemade rockets for fun. One time he told the class he was working on a new kind of rocket fuel—a solid fuel, something more powerful and advanced than anything NASA had come up with.

"You mean he has a secret formula?" Scott asked.

Jenny nodded. "I think that's exactly it. Then, later, another kid asked a question about it, and he said he shouldn't have brought it up in the first place, and we should all forget he mentioned it."

"So maybe we should forget it too," Mark said.

"My lips are sealed," said Scott.

Inspired by Mr. Drizzle, Jenny had followed the Apollo-Soyuz mission and watched the splashdown on TV the afternoon before.

"Lucky," Mark said.

"We read about it in the newspaper," Scott said.

"The astronauts almost died," Jenny said.

"Yeah—when that poison gas came in the spacecraft on re-entry," Mark said.

"Nitrogen tetroxide propellant from the RCS—reaction control system." Jenny pronounced all that like it was easy. "They forgot to close a valve or something."

Scott and Mark looked at each other, then at Jenny, who had turned pink. "Sorry," she said. "My friends call me an egghead."

"Jenny the egghead," Scott said.

"'Egg' for short," Mark said.

"Jenny!" Jenny's mom appeared at the head of the path through the trees. She was walking with Grandpa. "Oh, there you are. Time to go, honey. Did you have a nice time?"

"I dunno, Mom." She looked at Mark and Scott. "Did we have a nice time?"

The boys cracked up, which Jenny's mom interpreted as yes.

"Told you so," she said to her daughter and then to the boys, "Come back later in the summer, why don't you? Maybe you kids can get together again."

CHAPTER 4

If Mom and Dad had driven up at that moment, the week would have ended on a happy note. Unfortunately, Scott and Mark's parents weren't due till the next morning . . . and after dinner, things kind of went to heck.

Jenny's mom had left the blueberry pie, and Scott was bringing it to the table for dessert. Later, Mark said he didn't know why he did what he did. It was just one of those irresistible ideas that come into your head. Every morning, Grandpa put the rubber band from the newspaper in a plastic dish on the windowsill by the kitchen table. The dish was overflowing with rubber bands. Mark's idea was grab one and shoot it at his brother's head.

"*Ow!*"

A direct hit—*yes!*

But Mark's satisfaction didn't last. Scott swiped at his stinging ear, the pie fell to the floor, and the plate broke, shooting glass and blueberry goo everywhere. This was bad enough, but then things got worse. Barefoot, Scott stepped hard on a piece of glass, which neatly sliced his foot.

"*Aiiiii!*" he squealed as red ooze joined the purple stain on his heel.

Grandpa was up in a flash to examine Scott's injury. Then he ordered Mark to get the first-aid kit from the bathroom and maneuvered Scott onto the sofa so he could elevate his bleeding foot.

While Grandpa cleaned and bandaged the cut, Scott squeezed his eyes shut and willed his tears to stay put in his eyeballs. "Is it gonna get infected?" he asked.

"Hard telling with a blueberry wound," Grandpa said. "You might turn purple. You might not."

Meanwhile, Mark swept up the mess, did the dinner dishes, and dried them—all without being asked.

Chores done, Mark approached his brother, who was still on the sofa. "Does it hurt a lot?"

"What do you think?" Scott said.

"You might look good purple," Mark said. "And then people could tell us apart."

"Easy for you to look on the bright side," Scott said.

"Boys?" their grandpa said. By this time he had made himself comfortable on his beat-up recliner and was reading the dregs of the morning newspaper.

"I didn't mean to hurt him," Mark said.

"You shot a rubber band at my head," Scott reminded him.

"Yeah, okay. But I didn't mean to hurt your *foot*," Mark said.

Grandpa cleared his throat. "I can't help but notice that whenever you two are around, there's a high level of conflict."

The twins couldn't really argue with that.

"And a correspondingly high level of destruction."

Given the state of Scott's foot, not to mention the vivid purple stain on the linoleum floor, they couldn't argue there, either.

"Now, do you boys think that's a good thing?"

"No, sir," they said.

"So the question becomes, what ought we—meaning *you*—do about it?"

The boys mumbled variations of "We don't know, Grandpa." Then Mark added, "Do you have any suggestions?"

It so happened that he did. "I've just been reading about the Apollo-Soyuz mission you boys are so interested in. You know, up till now, the United States and the Soviet Union have been bitter enemies. The two countries' working together on this huge scientific project is a step forward for world peace."

Mark tried to follow his grandfather's logic. "So you're saying that since Scott and I act like enemies sometimes, we should rendezvous in space?"

"I'm saying why not work together on something constructive? You're great kids who can do anything you set your minds to. What if you built a go-kart or something?"

Scott and Mark liked the idea of a project. When they were five, they had stayed up to watch Neil Armstrong walk on the moon. Back then, they both wanted to be astronauts. But when they started school it turned out to be boring, and they didn't do that well, and their teachers didn't think they were that smart. So the dream of exploring space had faded. Now, as Grandpa spoke, it came back.

Scott said, "I'd rather build a spaceship than a go-kart."

Mark nodded. "Me too. And maybe that Egg girl can help us. Didn't she say her teacher has some kind of secret formula?"

"*Shhhh!*" Scott said.

"Egg girl?" Grandpa repeated.

"Jenny," Mark said.

Grandpa looked puzzled, but didn't ask for an explanation. Instead, he said, "Suit yourselves. Go on and build a spaceship in that case." Then he looked back at his newspaper. "And if you need any help, let me know."

Mark had had a brainstorm. "Well, actually, Grandpa,

what if you let us use your workshop?"

Grandpa shifted in his chair, but kept his eyes on the newspaper. "We'll see," he said.

The boys grinned at each other. In Grandpa-speak, that meant yes.

CHAPTER 5

....

"How do you build a spaceship, anyway?" Mark asked his brother.

He and Scott were lying in their own beds at home on Sunday morning. They could hear their dad making pancakes in the kitchen. They knew it was their dad because Mom had worked the swing shift—four to midnight—and would still be sleeping. She was a police officer too, the first woman on their town's force.

"It might be pretty hard," Scott said. "I think we need a whole lot of gasoline. It burns up and the fire pushes the spacecraft into space."

Mark rolled his eyes. "Don't be an idiot. Anybody knows you don't put gasoline in a rocket ship."

"Okay, genius," Scott said, "what do you put in it?"

"Rocket fuel," said Mark. "Like what Egg's teacher invented."

"And just how is that different from gasoline?" Scott asked.

"Well, it's obviously way different because, uh . . . it just is. And I think you're right that we need a lot. What else do we need?"

"Metal," said Scott.

"And where do we get metal?" Mark climbed out of bed and stretched.

"You have a bad attitude, you know that?" Scott sat up. "We'll find it. Maybe Grandpa's got extra in his workshop. He's got everything else."

"I just think it might be a good idea to have a plan first," said Mark.

In their hearts, Mark and Scott were as messy as any eleven-year-old boys anywhere. But unlike Grandpa, their parents wouldn't tolerate chaos. For that reason, the twins' bedroom looked tidy—provided you didn't pay a visit to the dust bunnies under the bed or scrutinize the depths of the clothes closet.

Now Mark tugged the corners of his red comforter so that it was more or less straight and punched his pillow. Scott, whose comforter was navy blue, did the same. Then they pulled on clean T-shirts over their pajama bottoms and went out to the kitchen to see how breakfast was coming.

"Sheesh, I thought you boys'd never get up," Dad said by way of greeting. "You're burnin' daylight, you know that?"

Mark wrinkled his nose. "Better than burning pancakes, Dad."

Scott laughed. "Good one."

"Hmph." With a spatula, Dad looked under the edge of a pancake on the griddle. "Nothing wrong with this one that syrup won't cure. Set the table, you two. And get out the milk. Oh—and Major Nelson's been wondering where his breakfast is, too."

Major Nelson, under the kitchen table, thumped his tail.

After breakfast, the boys cleaned up, and then they had a whole glorious summer day at their disposal. Usually, that would mean riding bikes before it got too hot, but to Mark's astonishment, Scott disappeared into the den and came back out with a yellow legal pad.

"Wait—I'm gonna ask Mom for the thermometer," Mark said. "You must be sick."

"Very funny, loser," said Scott. "I'm just doing what you said—making a plan. Turns out it wasn't that dumb of an idea. To make a spaceship, we need metal. What else?"

CHAPTER 6

Mark sat down beside his brother on the living room sofa. Major Nelson trotted in from the kitchen, circled twice, and dropped to his favorite spot on the carpet.

"A parachute," Mark said.

"In case the astronaut has to bail out?" Scott said.

"No, to slow the spaceship down when it's time to land," said Mark. "And then I think we need a second one that floats it back to Earth."

"Back to Greenwood Lake, you mean," said Scott. "That's where we're going to splash down."

"And we need electrical wiring for the controls. And a heat shield," said Mark.

Scott looked up. "A what?"

"I read it in *Life* magazine." Mark shrugged. "I'm not sure what it is, exactly, but it keeps the spaceship from burning like an overcooked pancake when it's coming back through the atmosphere."

Scott wrote it down. "Sounds important. Anything else?"

"A window," said Mark. "And a periscope. That way you can see all around, like out of a submarine."

"Oh yeah," said Scott. "It would be pretty crazy to go all that way and not see anything."

"A spacesuit," said Mark. "A camera. Air tanks. Hoses."

Scott was writing feverishly, then looked up. "Switches, cables, fuses, circuit breakers . . ."

Mark nodded. "Yeah, keep writing. And something else—a fire extinguisher."

Scott didn't want to think about a fire extinguisher, but he wrote it down just the same. Like his brother, he was well aware of the Apollo 1 disaster in 1967, when three astronauts died in a fire in a capsule still on the launchpad.

"We need a radio, too," Scott said, "to talk to Mission Control."

"Mission Control can be Egg's job," Mark said.

"What if she wants to go into space? Be an astronaut?" Scott asked.

Mark shook his head. "Girls can't be astronauts."

"Maybe they can," Scott said. "Some people say girls can't be cops either, but look at Mom."

Mark thought about that. "Ye-a-a-ah—but NASA doesn't take girl astronauts."

"There's a first time for everything," Scott said. "So maybe Egg will fly with us and be the first—only no one will know, because the whole thing's a secret."

"You bet it will be a secret," Mark said. "What if our friends found out we flew in space with a *girl*? It would be over for us."

This made both boys laugh, but it also raised an important question. How many astronauts could their spaceship hold? And who would they be? Each twin was sure about one thing. If he was going to do all the work to build a spaceship, he was definitely going up in space.

Scott flexed his fingers, which were tired from so much writing, and showed the list to his brother. His handwriting was small and neat. Mark usually made fun of him for it. But now it made the list look good—a good first step for their project.

In fact, the twins agreed it was such a good first step that they could take the rest of the day off. They stood up to go out to the garage and get their bikes. Major Nelson stood up too, and wagged his tail.

"Sorry, Nelson." Mark scratched the dog behind his ears. "But you have to stay inside."

Major Nelson and bicycles were not a good combination. For some reason, the dog seemed to think the only good bicycle was one that had been chased, knocked down, and flattened.

"By the way, what kind of spaceship are we building?" Scott asked as he and Mark headed out.

"We should keep it simple," Mark said, "so maybe, like, a Mercury spacecraft. The Mercury program was the first to send Americans into space, starting with Alan Shepard in 1961."

Scott rolled his eyes. "Do you have to be such a know-it-all?"

"I can't help it if I'm the smart one," Mark said. "Just like you can't help it you got dropped on your head. Anyway, the early Mercury flights were short. John Glenn's was just three orbits. A short flight would solve another problem I was thinking of."

"What?" Scott asked.

"The bathroom problem. I mean, who wants to wear diapers in space?"

"Ewww!" Scott grimaced. "Not me."

CHAPTER 7

When Mark and Scott were home in West Orange, their favorite pastime—even better than fighting with each other, getting in trouble, or taking stuff apart—was riding bikes. Like all their friends, they had Schwinn Sting-Rays—low-slung one-speeds with banana seats. The bikes, both purple, had been a birthday gift from their parents the year before. The Kellys had figured that if the bikes were identical, the twins would not be able to fight over them.

Wrong.

What they fought about was which bike belonged to which twin, disputes that ended only after Mark crashed his on the steep hill at the end of the block, leaving it dented, scarred, and easily identified.

Now, still in their own driveway, the twins saw that their neighbor Lori was on the sidewalk riding her new birthday bike, her mom hovering over her. Lori had just turned five, and her pink bike had training wheels.

"You're doing great, Lori," Mark said.

Concentrating too hard to look up, Lori said, "Thank you very much." Her mom smiled and waved.

The twins circled once, then took off down Greenwood Avenue toward their friend Barry Leibovitz's house.

As they raced by, another neighbor—Mr. Frank—backed his big white sedan out of his driveway.

"MiG at two o'clock!" Scott called to his brother.

"I've got him in my sights!" Mark answered.

"Go for missile lock—"

"I'm too close! I'm going to guns—"

The white car turned and came down the street behind them.

"He's on your tail!"

"Brake hard and he'll fly by—"

"Closing . . . closing . . . *ratta-tat-tat!*" Mark pumped his fist as Mr. Frank, little knowing he'd been shot down, drove by and waved.

In Barry's driveway, the bikes lurched to a stop and the boys vaulted over the front-porch railing. They were going to ring the bell, but Barry opened the door and said, "Greetings, earthlings!"

Barry was into science fiction.

"Hey, come out and ride with us—can you?" Mark asked.

"I think," Barry said. "My parents aren't home. Let me tell my brother."

Barry's big brother, Tommy, had been an Air Force pilot in the Vietnam War. While flying a secret mission he still couldn't talk about, he had been shot down and held prisoner for months. Now that the war was finally over, he was living with his family till he could find a job and a place of his own.

Tommy was slouched on the sofa in the living room, watching a *Beverly Hillbillies* rerun. Since leaving the Air Force, he had let his hair grow long, and he had a beard. He was wearing a tie-dyed T-shirt, jeans, and sandals. One time Mark had heard his mom say it was a good thing she knew Tommy Leibovitz was a war hero or she would've taken him for a hippie.

Tommy looked up when the three boys came in. "What's happenin'?"

Barry explained he wanted to ride bikes.

Tommy nodded. "Cool." Then he looked back at the TV.

"Is your brother okay?" Scott asked when they were all outside.

Barry shrugged. "I guess. Mom says he's been through a lot and we have to cut him some slack."

"I like his stories about flying," said Mark. "We wouldn't know anything about being a pilot except for him."

"Does he ever talk about being in the Air Force? A POW?" Scott asked.

"Not too much," Barry said. "All I know is, he was imprisoned in someplace called the Hanoi Hilton. It sounds like a hotel, but I guess it wasn't so nice."

"Come on"—Mark jumped on his bike—"where are we goin' today?"

....

CHAPTER 8

The three boys cruised around town, racing one another, shooting Russian missiles out of the sky, and popping wheelies till they were too hot and sweaty to continue.

"A root beer float would taste pretty good about now," Mark said as they coasted past the Dairy Queen on Pleasant Valley Way.

"Too bad we're still payin' Dad back for the calculator," Scott said.

"I've got money," said Barry. "You can owe me."

"No lie?" Mark made a sharp right so Barry couldn't change his mind.

The boys parked their bikes by the restaurant door and locked them together.

"My mom pays me to balance her checkbook," Barry explained.

"I knew you were good at math," Scott said as they walked inside, "but I didn't know you were that good."

"Balancing a checkbook is arithmetic, not math," said Barry.

"There's a difference?" Mark said.

"Arithmetic is just keeping track of figures like what an adding machine can do," Barry said. "Math is more like a language to help you work with anything numbers describe."

Scott raised his eyes to heaven. "Help!" he cried. "I'm surrounded by know-it-alls!"

Mark slapped his brother on the back. "You're probably good at something. And someday, if you're lucky, we'll find out what."

Scott slugged his brother's arm, and Barry laughed.

The root beer floats were forty-five cents. Barry ordered three and paid for them. Then the boys sat down at a table inside so they could enjoy the air-conditioning. When Barry asked about Greenwood Lake, the twins told him they'd done a whole lot of chores for their grandpa.

"Sounds brutal. Didn't you have any fun?" Barry asked.

"We're going back next week, and then we'll have fun. We've got this project we're working on," said Mark.

"What project?" Barry asked at the same time Scott was signaling, *What gives? It's a secret!*

"Oh yeah," Mark responded to his brother. "Never mind," he told Barry.

"Hey—no fair," said Barry. "Didn't I just lend you guys money?"

"He's got a point," Mark said to his brother, who was slurping the last of his melted ice cream.

"Plus we're planning to tell Egg," Scott said.

"You've got a friend named Egg?" Barry said. "Weird."

"Worse yet, she's a girl," said Mark.

"Double weird," said Barry. "But what's the secret?"

Mark and Scott took turns explaining, and were annoyed when Barry's response was to laugh so uncontrollably that everyone else at the Dairy Queen looked over to see if he was having a fit.

"Do you have any idea how hard that would be?" Barry asked after he had calmed down. "It took NASA four years to put a man in space, and they had millions of dollars and hundreds of scientists and engineers."

"That's the point," said Mark. "NASA already figured out how. All we have to do is copy. Same as Scott does in school."

Scott ignored the insult. Barry shook his head. "As my grandmother would say, *Oy vey!* You guys have a lot to learn."

Listening, Scott momentarily felt like an idiot. Maybe he and his brother were crazy. Maybe they should just give up and build a go-kart. But then he had another thought.

"Mark and I don't know that much about math. But you do. How about if you come with us to Grandpa's and help?"

"Hey, yeah!" Mark said. "Grandpa wouldn't mind. And there's plenty of room in Twin Territory."

Barry said that sounded good, even if he didn't have a lot of confidence in Mark and Scott's project. Barry loved his brother, but Tommy's homecoming had been an adjustment for the family. Barry wouldn't mind a vacation.

CHAPTER 9

Mark and Scott wanted to telephone Egg to make a plan for their next visit to Greenwood Lake and tell her about the project. Maybe they'd even read her the list they made. But their parents vetoed a phone call.

"It's long-distance, the toll charges are expensive, and you guys are still in debt," Dad said that night at dinner. "Why not write her a letter? Stamps only cost ten cents."

Mark and Scott looked at one another. The only letters they ever wrote were birthday and Christmas thank-you notes.

"How long would a letter take to get to Greenwood Lake?" Mark asked.

"If you mail it Monday morning, it will be there on Tuesday," Dad said. "I can get the address from your grandfather."

"But you'll have to phone him to get it!" Mark said. "So in that case, why can't we just—"

"Because I have to call Grandpa anyway," Dad said. "And because I'm the one who pays the phone bill."

Mom looked up from her spaghetti. "Excuse me?"

"Correction," Dad said. "Your mom *and* I pay the phone bill. And all the other bills, too."

After dinner, Scott and Mark were watching *Emergency!*, one of their favorite shows, when Dad came into the living room and handed them a slip of paper with Jenny O'Malley's address on it. After the show was over, Scott copied the list they had made that morning onto a fresh sheet of yellow legal paper, and Mark wrote the letter:

> Dear Egg, also known as Egghead, also known
> as Jenny,
>
> My brother and I think you might be able to
> help us with a project. If you're interested, I mean.
> We think you might be helpful because, like you
> said, you are an egghead. We are not. Anyway,
> what it is is building a spaceship like a Mercury
> spacecraft that orbits Earth one time. We think it
> could blast off from somewhere around our grand-
> pa's house and splash down in the lake.
>
> We could work on it next time we visit
> Grandpa. We hope next week. Is next week okay?

Our friend Barry is going to help, too. He is also an egghead.

Scott wrote the list of stuff we think we will need. I guess there might be more, too. It is in the envelope with this letter.

There is one more thing. We don't think we should tell any grown-ups about it. Grown-ups might think it is a bad idea. However, Grandpa doesn't count. He thought of it in the first place.

Do you want to work on this project with us?

Yours truly,

Mark Kelly

Scott had made some suggestions while Mark was writing, and now he read the letter over, frowned, and suggested a PS, which Mark added:

P.S.—It is okay if you don't want to.

Mom mailed the letter on her way to work on Monday morning.

On Tuesday they checked the mailbox in front of their house, even though Mom and Dad both told them it was physically impossible for Egg to have answered that fast. Then, on Wednesday, they checked again and sure enough, there was a letter addressed to Mark and Scott Kelly!

Egg's handwriting was as neat as Scott's, but bigger and rounder. They were glad she hadn't used pink ink or smelly stationery. It was just a plain letter in blue ink on lined paper.

Dear Mark and Scott,

I would like to help you with the project. If you can come to Greenwood Lake next Wednesday and stay a few days, that would be good. We can go to the library to do research.

I understand about not telling grown-ups. But I have a question. After the project is all done, would it be okay if I submitted it for the annual school science fair? In my grade the same kid, Steve Peluso, gets a blue ribbon every single year, and I am sick of it. If our spaceship works, I think I, for once, might beat him.

Sincerely,

Jenny O'Malley (also known as Egg)

P.S.—We need a name for the project. Here is my suggestion: *Project Blastoff*.

"Project Blastoff," Mark repeated. "I like it!"

Scott agreed. "And it's okay if she wants to enter it in the science fair after we've already been to space."

Mark nodded. "Because by then, no grown-up can stop us!"

CHAPTER 10

The following Wednesday morning, Mom drove Mark, Scott, and Barry to Greenwood Lake. The car had barely come to rest in Grandpa's driveway when the car doors burst open and the boys piled out and ran up the walk, shoving each other and laughing.

"Nice to see you boys so enthused," Mom said as she followed them into the empty house. Grandpa's car was outside, so they knew he was around somewhere.

"We've got big plans for our visit," Mark told their mom.

"Something to do with that girl named Egg—the one you wrote to?" Mom asked.

Scott was afraid Mark wouldn't be able to resist bragging about the project, so he punched him.

"*Ow!* What was that for?" Mark rubbed his arm. "I'm not gonna say anything."

"Secrets, huh?" Mom said. The three boys climbed the ladder to Twin Territory and dumped their duffel bags.

"Not *secrets*, exactly," Scott said.

"A project," Mark said.

In the summer, it was always hot in the loft, so Scott turned on the fan, which kicked up a whirlwind of dust. Mom had followed them partway up the ladder and was looking over the top rung. "I see one project you can do—cleaning up in here."

"I knew it!" said Barry. "The chores are starting already."

"Don't scare him, Mom," said Scott.

"Anyway, after lunch, Egg's coming over and we're going to the library," said Mark.

Mom closed her eyes and shook her head. "I'm sorry. There must be something wrong with my ears. For a second I actually thought you said 'library.'"

"He did say 'library,'" Mark said.

Mom looked from one twin to the other, then finally at Barry. "What have you done to my sons?"

Barry laughed. "Don't blame me. I think it's that girl named Egg."

"I am still getting used to that idea—a girl named Egg," Mom said.

Scott said, "Egg explained we have to go to the library because of, uh . . . the stuff we're doing."

"But it's one time only." Mark gripped the wooden railing at the edge of the loft, swung himself over, and dropped to the floor—*thump*—the preferred method of leaving Twin Territory.

Scott was right behind him—*thump*. "We promise it will never happen again."

Barry looked doubtfully over the edge. "Do I have to jump?"

"No, but if you don't, Mark will make fun of you," Scott said.

Barry sighed. "Very well." He turned, grabbed the railing, closed his eyes and jumped—*thuh-bump*.

Mom was climbing down the ladder when the front door swung open. "Welcome, welcome!" Grandpa came in carrying a paper bag filled with bell peppers from the garden. "Good to see you. Anybody hungry? I've got peanut butter."

"With peppers?" Mom said.

"Peanut butter goes with everything," Grandpa said.

Mark and Scott introduced Grandpa to Barry. Then sandwiches were made, and they all sat down at the table for lunch.

Mom and Grandpa pronounced peanut butter and bell pepper sandwiches a culinary delight, but the three boys ate their peppers on the side.

When lunch was over, Mom gave each twin a hug, which each twin tried to wiggle out of. Then she squeezed Barry's shoulder, said good-bye to Grandpa, and left to drive back to West Orange.

"Is Jenny coming over to work on the project?" Grandpa asked when Mom was gone.

Mark said, "We call her 'Egg.'"

"And I call her Jenny," Grandpa said.

Scott said, "We're going to the library—and you don't need to make fun of us, because Mom already did."

"I would never make fun of you for going to the library!" Grandpa said. "It's a repository of all human knowledge."

"Yeah, that's the problem," said Mark. "But we still have to go, because we need to do research before we start building."

Egg's mom drove up to the house a few minutes later, and Egg jumped out of the car with a grin on her face. Mark and Scott were glad to see her, too. Even though they hadn't known her long, she seemed like an old friend.

"Hi, Mr. Kelly! Hi, guys!" Egg greeted them. "And you must be Barry. Great to meet you."

"Same," said Barry.

Egg's mom, Mrs. O'Malley, rolled down the driver's-side window. "I hope you don't mind if I don't get out of the car, Joe. I've got a meeting later, and I need to move along. Are you kids ready?"

"Do we need to bring anything?" Mark asked.

"I've got it covered," Egg said.

The library was in the town of West Milford, a fifteen-minute drive from Grandpa's house. It was quiet in the car. The boys were bursting to talk about the project, but they couldn't say anything in front of Egg's mom.

"Are you having a good summer?" Mrs. O'Malley asked.

"Yes, ma'am," said Mark. Scott nodded.

"What have you been doing since I last saw you?" Mrs. O'Malley asked.

"Nothing much," said Mark. Scott shrugged.

"Jenny's been very busy," Mrs. O'Malley said.

"They call me 'Egg,'" Egg explained to her mom. "It's short for 'egghead.' They think I'm a brain."

Mrs. O'Malley laughed. "I hope that's a good thing."

Scott said, "Barry's kind of a brain, too."

"No, I'm not," Barry said.

"So you have something in common," Mark said.

"No, we don't," Barry said.

Laughing, Mrs. O'Malley turned the car into a parking lot by a brick building with a flag in front. "I'll meet you here in a couple of hours," she said.

A couple of hours? Mark and Scott looked at each other. In their minds, a visit to the library meant pulling one or two books off the shelf. What could possibly take such a long time?

"Sounds good." Egg climbed out of the car with an empty canvas book bag over her shoulder. The boys were right behind her.

But wait.

At the bottom of the steps that led to the library's entrance stood another kid, and now Egg was saying hello to him like they'd planned to meet all along. Scott and Mark looked at each other. Who the heck was this?

CHAPTER 11

The boy was named Howard Chin. He was going into seventh grade at Egg's school. Scott, Mark, and Barry learned all this in about ten seconds. What they didn't learn was what he was doing there.

Howard's clothes looked normal enough—jeans and a T-shirt—but he didn't smile and he had something weird clipped to his belt: a long orange case.

"What the heck is that supposed to be?" Scott whispered to Barry as they walked up the steps.

"Slide rule," Barry said.

"What's a slide rule?" Mark wanted to know.

"It's a special ruler you can do math calculations on," Barry explained. "Howard must be a math nerd like me."

"We don't need *two* math nerds," said Scott.

The library was about the size of a large house. It had

scuffed beige linoleum floors and white walls. Just inside the entrance, a lone librarian stood behind a wooden checkout desk. She had been ink-stamping returned books, but when the kids walked in, she looked up. "Hello, Jenny! Did you already finish reading the books from last week? And who are your friends?"

"I didn't finish all of them yet." Jenny introduced the boys and said, "Can you tell me where the physics books are?"

"Oh dear. We're not very long in physics," the librarian said. "For that, you'd need a university library. But if it's the basics you're after, they're in 530–539. That's up the stairs in the row nearest the south wall."

"How about the encyclopedia?" Barry asked.

"Good idea," said Jenny, "and I know where that is."

On the library's second floor, the five kids found several long tables with chairs around them, an orange vinyl sofa, and row after row of bookcases. Half a dozen grown-ups were sitting at the tables, reading, writing, or both. There were several people in the children's section, which was in an alcove to the left of the stairs.

Mark and Scott knew from school that 530–539 referred to numbers in the Dewey Decimal System, an organizing scheme that numbers every nonfiction book according to its subject. Since each row of bookcases was labeled with the numbers of the books it contained, it was easy to find what they wanted.

"How about this one?" Egg pulled a book called *Fundamentals of Modern Physics* off the shelf.

Mark nodded. "Looks great."

On a nearby shelf that held the 600s, mechanical engineering, Howard spotted another helpful-looking book, *Theory of Flight*.

Scott looked at his brother, then at Egg. "Uh . . . can I ask a question?"

Egg said, "Shoot—except we're in a library, so you have to speak softly."

"Okay. Why do we need to know physics, anyway?"

Howard snorted, then covered his mouth with his hand. "Sorry."

Mark and Scott had the same thought at the same time. Howard was tall but skinny. They could take him easy, and Barry would help. On the other hand, it probably wasn't cool to pulverize somebody in a library.

"One of the things physics explains is how things like spaceships move and what makes them move," Egg answered. "So if we want to figure out how to make a rocket move upward and into orbit, then we have to understand some physics. There's actually a lot we need to know, but we can start with Newton's Three Laws of Motion."

"That's Sir Isaac Newton," said Mark.

"Really?" said Scott. "I thought it was his younger brother, Fig."

Everybody laughed at that—even Howard.

The boys took their books to an empty table. Then Egg brought over a volume of the encyclopedia. Everybody sat down. Egg pulled notebook paper and pens out of her bag and distributed them.

"Okay, so we've all got our books and our paper and our pens," she said.

"Check, check, and check," said Mark.

"So we're interested in Newton's Laws. What if we all read up on them and talk about it later to make sure we understand. I mean"—all of a sudden, she looked embarrassed—"if that's okay. I'm not trying to be the boss or anything."

Mark said, "Yeah, you are. But for now that's okay. You brought the pens and paper."

After that, everybody read and took notes. The books were written for adults. The print was small, there were a ton of words on every page, and some of the words and ideas were tough to understand. But Mark and Scott really wanted Project Blastoff to work, so they read and reread till things started to make sense.

"Can I say something?" Barry asked.

Egg nodded.

"My butt hurts," Barry said. "These chairs are hard."

The guys all cracked up, and Egg rolled her eyes. "I guess we have been sitting for a while."

Mark looked at the clock on the wall and couldn't believe it was almost four.

"All the books except the encyclopedia circulate," said Egg. "Let's take them outside to talk so we don't bother anybody."

Downstairs, Egg used her library card to check out the books. "Are you starting early for the big science fair, dear?" the librarian asked her.

Egg hesitated and finally said, "Uh, maybe."

The librarian laughed. "Don't worry. I won't say a word to the Pelusos. What kind of project is it, if you don't mind my asking?"

Mark answered before Egg had a chance. "Secret," he said.

"Oh!" The librarian looked at him, then at Egg. "Well, just so you don't blow anything up."

CHAPTER 12

On their way to the park, Jenny had a crazy idea. "Wouldn't it be great if we could get all the information in the library at home? Maybe it could be transmitted like television," she said. "Then we wouldn't have to lug these heavy books around, or worry about not being able to keep an encyclopedia volume."

"It would be great if I had wings, too," said Mark, "but that doesn't mean it's gonna happen."

"Actually," said Barry, "computer processors get smaller all the time. There's something called Moore's Law that predicts eventually they'll be small enough so you could carry a computer in your pocket."

Howard nodded. "And the military has been experimenting with linking computers together with phone lines to form a giant database. If that database were made available to the public, anybody could see a library's worth of information from anywhere."

"Ha!" said Scott. "That's just science fiction talking. Hey—how about if we sit at that table?"

The picnic table Scott pointed to was in the shade of an elm tree. The five kids arranged themselves on the benches. Egg took the big science and physics books she'd been carrying out of her book bag. "So after we're done orbiting the Earth," she said, "maybe we can work on creating a giant electronic library available to everyone. In the meantime, who wants to say what he found out about physics?"

"Me," said Mark.

"There's a surprise," said Scott.

Mark ignored him. "Sir Isaac Newton was born in England in 1642 and died in England in 1727. One day, while he was still alive, an apple fell on his head, and—"

"The story of Newton and the apple is made up. It's a myth," Howard interrupted.

Barry said, "Maybe not. And anyway, it's a good story."

Mark gave Howard a dirty look. "Like I was saying, his bruised head made him think about why the apple fell, and all of a sudden he realized that large objects like the Earth pull other things to them, and that pull is caused by gravity."

"Small objects have gravity, too," Howard said. "But how much they have is proportional to their mass, so massive objects like Earth have more."

Mark frowned. He didn't like being corrected.

Meanwhile, Scott said, "I thought we were talking about three laws."

"The first one is the law of inertia," Mark said. "According to it, an object at rest will stay at rest until a force moves it."

"That one made sense to me," Scott said, "because I happen to know from personal observation that our dad lazing around on the sofa will stay lazing around on the sofa until a powerful force—like our mom—makes him get up."

"There's another part of the first law too," Mark said. "Once something's moving, it stays moving, unless a force slows it down."

"Yeah, and that part *didn't* make sense to me," said Scott, "because I also happen to know that if I throw a baseball and no one catches it, it doesn't fly forever. It would be cool if it did, though."

"Actually, it would be kind of dangerous," said Barry. "Everybody'd always be getting hit with escaped baseballs, footballs, Frisbees, old javelins from King Arthur's time . . ."

Egg and Howard started to explain at the same time why flying javelins aren't much of a threat, but Scott stopped them. "Slow down a sec, would you? I already feel stupid."

"You're not stupid. It was a good question," Egg said.

"Oh, come on," said Mark. "He's at least a little bit stupid."

"Scott doesn't seem that stupid to me," said Howard.

"Thanks . . . I think," Scott said. Then he looked at his brother. "If you know so much, you explain it."

"Uhhh . . . ," said Mark.

"Thought so," said Scott.

Egg tried again. "There are two forces that stop the baseball, but they're both so familiar that they're easy to forget—gravity and friction."

"Okay, I get gravity," said Scott. "We already covered it, plus it's the reason a high fly ball doesn't go to Jupiter. But friction means rubbing against something. What's the baseball rubbing against?"

"The air," Egg explained. "Think of air like water, because in a lot of ways it is. If you threw a baseball in water, the water would resist, and the baseball wouldn't get far. Air is the same thing only not as dense, so it doesn't slow things down as much."

Scott nodded. "Okay. I think I am now officially ready for the second law."

Mark opened his mouth, but Howard was faster. "Force equals mass times acceleration, which can also be expressed as the equation $F=ma$."

Barry nodded.

Everybody else just looked at Howard, who finally shrugged. "There's nothing else to explain. That's it."

"Maybe for *you*," Mark said. Then he looked at Barry. "You want to try that in regular human-speak?"

Barry said, "Going back to throwing a baseball, the force is how hard your arm pushes it, the mass is the ball, and the acceleration is, well . . . acceleration."

"The rate at which the ball's speed speeds up," Egg said.

Howard added, "Another way to say that is, the rate of change of its momentum."

Mark had had just about enough of Howard showing off how smart he was. The kid was weird. Why didn't he ever smile? How come Egg had even brought him?

Scott closed his eyes and tugged his short hair. "You're all giving me a headache. But I think it makes sense. How hard you throw the baseball, and the mass of the baseball, determines how fast the baseball accelerates."

"Mass is the same as size, right?" Mark said.

"Sort of," Barry said. "Mostly when we say size, we think of volume. So the volume of a beach ball is bigger than the volume of a baseball, but a baseball is more massive—"

"—because it's heavier," said Mark. "I get it."

Egg shook her head. "Not exactly. Mass is more like

the amount of stuff in stuff. Remember that the idea of 'heavy' relates to gravity, and in space gravity's force is less than on Earth. So the weight of something changes when it's in space, or on the Moon, or on Earth, but its mass is always the same."

"There's an equation that describes mass," said Barry.

"I was afraid of that," said Scott.

"Mass equals density times volume—$M=D{\cdot}V$," Barry said.

"What Scott said about common sense is right," Egg said. "But you have to remember there are other influences on acceleration besides force and mass. There are also friction and gravity."

"Friction and gravity *again*?" said Mark.

"And because the second law is an equation, you can work it backward and sideways," said Barry.

"Try that one again," said Scott.

"If you know the mass of something and how fast it's accelerating, you can figure out how much force it took to move it. And if you know its acceleration and the amount of force that moved it, you can figure out its mass."

Scott nodded. "That's cool."

Barry said, "That's algebra."

"Really?" Scott said. "So now I know algebra?"

"Algebra just means using variables—like letters—to

solve problems. So if I say two *x* equals six, solve for *x*, then I've expressed an arithmetic problem as algebra," Barry said.

"X equals three," Mark said.

"My brother, the genius," Scott said.

Mark waved and bowed to an imaginary crowd of fans—"Thank you, thank you very much"—until Howard interrupted by saying, "I don't think Mark is a genius."

Mark was more surprised than insulted, but Scott and Barry both sat up, ready to pound the kid.

"Howard!" Egg said. "That was a joke!"

Howard looked from Scott to Barry, alarmed by their reaction. "It was?"

"Sometimes Howard doesn't get jokes," Egg explained.

"He got the one about Fig Newton," Mark said.

Keeping his eyes on Scott and Barry, Howard shook his head. "No, I didn't. I just laughed because everyone else did. A Fig Newton is a cookie, right? What does a cookie have to do with Sir Isaac Newton?"

"They have the same name," Barry said.

Howard nodded solemnly. "Yes."

Mark saw that the kid was genuinely confused. He's weird, all right, Mark thought. And kind of obnoxious, but maybe not on purpose. Then Mark thought of somebody on a TV show his parents used to watch, *Star Trek*. The character's name was Mr. Spock, and he never smiled. Howard reminded Mark of Mr. Spock.

Thinking of that, Mark felt less angry. "What's really insulting," he said, "is how you guys think the perfectly reasonable idea that I'm a genius is only a joke."

That made everybody laugh—Howard too. But Howard's laughter seemed nervous.

CHAPTER 13

"Remember how my butt was starting to hurt?" Barry said. "Well, it's happening again, not to mention I'm getting sweaty."

"Luckily, there's only one more law," said Egg. "For every action, there is an equal and opposite reaction."

Mark nodded. "So if I bounce a basketball on the ground, it bounces back up. I get it. Are we done?"

Egg frowned. "A basketball isn't a good example. There's gravity, friction, the effect of the compression of the air inside, the rubberized material . . ."

"Yeah," Scott said, "because in my personal experience, if you try to bounce a rock off the ground, it won't work. I think maybe Newton got the third law wrong." He shrugged. "But hey, he made a good effort. And two out of three isn't bad."

"It's not good enough to qualify you as a genius, though," Mark said, "and genius is something I happen to know about."

Howard pointed at Mark. "That was a joke. Wasn't it?"

Mark said, "There's hope for you yet, but can I ask a question? What are you doing here, anyway?"

Scott and Barry fidgeted.

Egg frowned angrily. "He's here because I invited him!"

"I know that," Mark said, "and I also know you invited him for a reason, so what was the reason?"

Howard did not seem bothered by the question. "My Altair 8800," he said. "Also, I know BASIC."

Scott looked at everybody else. "Translation?"

Egg explained. "An Altair 8800 is a computer that's small enough so you can have one at your house—and Howard does. BASIC is the name of a language for telling the computer what to do."

"Whoa," said Barry. "That is so cool. Did you put the 8800 together yourself or buy it preassembled?"

"I put it together," Howard said. "It wasn't hard."

Now Scott and Mark were paying attention. This Howard kid had assembled a real computer himself! That was way better than taking apart a calculator. They had a thousand questions, but before they could ask even one, Egg looked up and waved.

"My mom's here," she said. "We gotta go."

CHAPTER 14

Howard lived west of town, so Mrs. O'Malley gave him a ride to his dad's work, which was nearby on the highway at an auto repair place called Nando's.

"See you tomorrow at two?" Howard said to Egg when he opened the car door.

"Sounds good," said Egg. At the same time, a girl came out of Nando's office door and smiled and waved.

"Hang on a sec, Mom, could you?" Egg jumped out behind Howard and jogged over to talk to the girl.

"That's Lisa Perez," Mrs. O'Malley told Mark, Scott, and Barry. "She's in Howard's class at school, and it's her dad's shop."

Egg came back a few seconds later and climbed in. Howard turned to wave, but didn't smile.

"He doesn't like us," Scott said as they drove off

toward Grandpa Kelly's house. "And now we'll never get to fool around with his computer."

"I don't think it's that," Egg said. "He's just not a smiler."

"So, Egg, what is it you and your good friend Howard are doing tomorrow at two o'clock?" Mark asked.

"Library," Egg said, "just like you."

"Hey—wait a second," Mark said.

"You've got to be kidding!" Scott said. "Today was enough library to last me through summer, and possibly high school."

"Seriously?" said Egg. "You thought that was all the research we needed to do to build a—"

"*Egg!*" Mark waved to keep her from giving away the secret.

"—a science fair project," Egg concluded.

"You guys have to admit there's a lot we don't know yet," Barry said.

"Yeah," said Egg. "Like we should research the history of the space—"

"*Egg!*" Mark interrupted again.

Mrs. O'Malley laughed. "What if I just promise not to listen?"

Egg said, "Or what if everybody just agrees we'll go to the library again tomorrow? We can talk then."

Barry was in favor. Scott and Mark grumbled, but in the end said okay.

When Mrs. O'Malley pulled into Grandpa's drive-way, she said, "I trust you kids, so I'm glad to support the project you're working on. It's even okay—for now—if you don't want to give away secrets. However, I'd appreciate it if you promised me one thing."

"What's that, Mom?" Egg asked.

"Just please don't blow anything up."

"I wonder why everybody's so worried we'll blow something up," Mark said later. The three boys were clearing dinner dishes. Grandpa had grilled hot dogs, and they had eaten outside at a table on the flat patch of dirt that was supposed to become a patio one day. Now the boys were cleaning, and Grandpa was talking to someone—they didn't know who—on the telephone extension in his bedroom.

"I guess we just look dangerous," said Scott.

"Or"—Barry stuck out his tongue, rolled back his eyes, and waggled his fingers—"*crrrrr-azy!*"

In the kitchen, Scott turned on the water to start washing dishes. "Maybe they've figured out what the project is. It's kind of like blowing something up. There will be flammable fuel, and we'll ignite it to send the rocket into space."

"That's what Newton's Third Law is about, isn't it?" Mark asked.

Scott turned off the water; then both twins looked at Barry.

"Oh, I get it," Barry said. "With Egg and Howard gone, now I'm the resident brain."

Mark was quick to reassure him. "We think you're brainy even when Egg and Howard are around."

"Just not that brainy," said Scott.

"On the other hand," said Mark, "you do have two good qualities. First, you get jokes, and second, you're not a girl."

"Another thing I get is Newton's Third Law," said Barry, "which is key to understanding how rockets work."

Mark tossed him a dish towel. "You can explain while you dry the dishes."

"More chores." Barry sighed. "Hasn't your grandfather ever heard of this radical new invention, the dishwasher?"

"He says he doesn't need one for just one person, and if it's more than one person, it's us, and we're the dish-washers." Mark handed Barry a plate dripping with water.

Barry talked while he dried. "Rockets were actually invented by the Chinese hundreds of years ago, then improved on by the Indians—the East Indians, I mean— and the British."

Putting dishes away, Mark threw back his head and sang: "O-oh, say can you see-e-e, by the dawn's early light, what so proudly we hailed—"

Scott slapped his ears with his sudsy hands. "Make him stop!"

Barry laughed. "Yup, 'the rockets' red glare' in 'The Star-Spangled Banner' refers to British weapons fired in the War of 1812. Rockets were originally weapons and fireworks. The first guys to think of using them for space travel were science fiction writers like H. G. Wells and Jules Verne."

"Oh, *sure*—like I believe writers thought of that before scientists," Mark said. "You're just saying it because you like that science fiction stuff."

Scott turned the water off and pulled the stopper out of the sink. "I don't see why those writers thought a rocket would work best for going into space. Why not a giant slingshot powered by a giant rubber band? The astronaut climbs into a harness and *vrroooom!*—he's off in space."

"Except," Barry said, "accelerating to top speed instantly flattens his bones, not to mention all his organs, and"—Barry ran a finger over his throat—"no more astronaut."

"How about a giant ladder?" Mark asked.

"It wouldn't put you in orbit, for one thing," said Barry. "And besides, any ladder that tall would collapse under its own weight."

"I guess we're stuck with a rocket," said Scott.

"That's the best anybody's figured out so far, anyway,"

said Barry. "A rocket doesn't need atmosphere. It's a reaction engine, which means it works on the basis of Newton's Third Law—action–reaction. Action: the exhaust being pushed out by burning fuel. Reaction: the rocket going in the opposite direction."

Mark said, "And when you're blasting off, that direction is supposed to be up."

"Ye-a-a-ah, but only at the beginning," said Barry. "Once you get to the right altitude, you pitch over and the velocity shifts to horizontal so you can fly parallel to Earth's surface—in other words, you're put in a stable orbit. Galileo and Newton both devised equations describing the necessary velocity for orbiting a body or for escaping its gravitational pull—like if you want to go to the moon or Mars."

"Mars!" said Scott. "Hey, that's a great idea!"

Mark was equally enthusiastic.

But Barry waved the dish towel like a flag of surrender. "How about we stick to one thing at a time?"

CHAPTER 15

Since Grandpa didn't have a TV, the twins had to miss *Emergency!*, Mark's favorite show, that night. Instead, they lost to Grandpa at gin rummy while listening to the Yankees beat the Tigers on the radio. The next morning, they got dressed to go swimming after breakfast.

"What? No chores?" Barry said as they headed down the path to the water. "I thought we'd at least have to build a barn or clear a few acres of brush."

"That's later," Mark said.

"After we go to the library and improve our minds," said Scott.

"Hey"—Mark slapped Barry's shoulder—"we told you it'd be fun if you came with us to Greenwood Lake. Aren't you glad you're here?"

Barry grinned. "Sure. No matter how many chores we have to do, it's good not to be listening to my dad nagging my brother, and my mom nagging my dad for nagging my brother."

"Is it like that all the time?" Scott asked.

"Enough of the time," Barry said. "My dad was a pilot in Korea. He came back, went to work, then went to college at night on the GI Bill, which pays for school for veterans. He doesn't see why it should be any different now, but Joe says it is. I don't know who's right, so I stay clear of them when the subject comes up."

The path to the beach went by Grandpa's workshop, then through a patch of trees past a field that had been cleared for houses, and then through a mess of low-lying shrubs before going over a rise and arriving at a quiet beach. Mark sprinted for the water: "Last one in's a rotten egg!"

The boys swam for a while, then took Grandpa's rowboat out.

"Look—Newton's laws in action," Scott said as he used the oars to push the boat through the water.

"If it weren't for friction, you'd only have to row one time, and then we'd just keep going forever," Mark said.

"Sounds relaxing," said Scott.

"Doesn't gravity come into it, too?" Mark asked. "Why aren't we sinking?"

"Newton's Third Law," said Barry. "Action: The force of gravity pulls the boat down. Reaction: The water pushes it up."

"What keeps it from tipping over?" Mark asked.

"The center of gravity is in line with the center of buoyancy," Barry said.

"*Boy*-ancy! You mean as opposed to *girl*-ancy, right? Good thing we didn't invite Egg to come with us, or we'd sink," said Mark.

"I don't think that's what he meant," said Scott.

"The way the mass of the boat is balanced, the gravity acts on one particular point—that's the center of *gravity*," said Barry.

"Even I've heard of that," Mark said.

"Because you're a genius," said Scott.

"As is well-known," said Mark.

"Uh-huh," said Barry. "Anyway, the center of *buoyancy* is the center of gravity of the volume of water that the hull displaces—the water moved out of the way because the boat takes up the space where it used to be. The center of buoyancy needs to be above the center of gravity. Because if it isn't and they get out of line, the boat starts to tip. It will probably keep tipping, tipping over, and probably sink. So if you load too much weight high in the boat, this can happen and if there is a wave or something, it can tip the boat over."

"And you drown," said Scott. "*Glug-glug-glug.*"

"Speak for yourself," said Mark. "I'm a good swimmer."

It was almost lunchtime by then, and the three boys were hungry. Mark rowed back, and together they pulled the boat onto the beach. They were walking back along the path when Mark stopped in his tracks and looked around.

"Hang on a sec," he said. "What do you guys think of this as a launch site?"

They were standing in the bare field between the shrubs and the trees. Grandpa said a builder had brought in a bulldozer and cleared it to put up houses, but there was some problem with money so the project was on hold.

"It's a pretty big area," said Scott.

"Out of the way, too," said Barry.

"Nothing to blow up, either." Mark grinned. "I think it's perfect."

CHAPTER 16

Grandpa Joe did the library drop-off that day, and the pickup, too. "Peggy—that is, Mrs. O'Malley—shouldn't have to do all the chauffeuring," he explained.

As the kids had done the day before, they spent part of the afternoon in the library and the rest in the park. When they were finished, Scott sighed and pronounced it "three lost hours of my precious summer."

Mark punched him.

They dropped Egg off at her house in town and Howard at Nando's Auto Repair. Then Grandpa steered the car for home. "You guys are awfully quiet," he noted.

Riding in the back with his brother, Mark leaned his head against the seat. "That's because building a space-ship turns out to be harder than you'd think. Did you know NASA spent millions of dollars on the Mercury program?"

"What's your budget?" Grandpa asked.

"Negative numbers," Scott said. "We still owe Dad for the calculator."

Barry shook his head. "I am trying really hard not to say 'I told you so.' But if you think about it, *I told you so.*"

"Lucky you're in the front seat, or we'd pound you," Scott said.

"I wouldn't have said it if I *weren't* in the front seat," said Barry.

They drove for a few minutes in silence; then, in a voice like a stage actor's, Grandpa said: "We choose to go to the moon not because it is easy but because it is hard, because the goal will serve to organize and measure the best of our energies and skills, uh . . . something something . . . because the challenge is one we are willing to accept, one we are unwilling to postpone." He shrugged and said in his normal voice, "I'm paraphrasing."

Mark closed his eyes and shook his head. "Grandpa, my brain's so tired it aches, and now you start talking crazy. What was *that* about?"

"President Kennedy, right?" Barry asked.

Grandpa nodded and looked at Mark in the rearview mirror. "The president's point was that sometimes you do the hard thing because doing hard things is good for you."

Like Grandpa, Scott and Mark were usually optimistic. But the stuff they had learned at the library about NASA's Mercury program did make their project look either impossible or crazy, or maybe both.

Besides the budget, there was the matter of rocket fuel. The Atlas rocket that shot John Glenn's *Friendship 7* spacecraft into space carried almost thirteen tons of rocket fuel. Where were they going to get that, as well as a rocket big enough to contain it?

Finally, there was the matter of personnel. Given all the challenges involved, their best bet would be to make the mission as simple as possible, and as light. That meant one astronaut. But both Mark and Scott wanted to be the first kid in space. For all they knew, maybe Egg, Barry, and Howard all expected to be astronauts as well.

Who would get to go?

CHAPTER 17

After so much physical activity at the lake and mental activity at the library, the boys were exhausted. Back at the house, they plopped down on Grandpa's old, super-comfy sofa and closed their eyes.

"What time's dinner, Grandpa?"

"Soon as you want to make it," Grandpa said, and all three boys groaned.

Without opening his eyes, Mark said, "If we're cooking, it'll be Froot Loops with a generous side of Frosted Flakes. I hope that's okay with you."

Grandpa pretended to consider. "I'd hate to die of sugar poisoning. Here's an idea. I'll make dinner. You boys go out and take a look at my workshop. Maybe some of the odds and ends will prove inspirational."

Mark sat up in a hurry. "Seriously?"

But Scott sighed. "You're not going to let us give up, are you, Grandpa?"

"You can't give up now," Grandpa said, "not when the whole thing's going so well."

"Going well?" said Scott. "We just realized the whole thing is totally impossible!"

"True," said Grandpa. "But look at it this way. You haven't had a fight all day, and the level of destruction around the house is way down."

"Before we can start building, we need plans," said Barry. "Have you got any graph paper, Mr. McAvoy?"

"I do, and I've got something else, too," Grandpa said. He went into the bedroom where his desk was and came back with an old issue of *Life* magazine that had a diagram of John Glenn's *Friendship* 7 spacecraft.

"People said I was crazy to save this," said Grandpa, "but I knew it would come in handy one day."

Friendship 7 was the first American spacecraft to orbit Earth with an astronaut inside. It was made up of four parts. By far the tallest and heaviest were the two stages of the Atlas launch vehicle, the fuel-filled rocket whose entire job was to push the smallest part, the capsule containing the astronaut, up and into orbit.

While Grandpa started dinner, the boys studied the magazine pictures. Then Scott called into the kitchen, "Are you sure it's okay if we go out to the workshop, Grandpa?"

Mark punched his brother. "Don't ask a̲g̲. What if he says no this time?"

"I heard that, Mark, and yes, it's okay," said Grandpa. "Just don't—"

"—blow anything up!" the three boys chorused.

"Well, there's that." Grandpa appeared in the kitchen doorway. "But what I had in mind was something else. I haven't been out there in a while, so it's probably pretty dusty, and who knows but some critters might have taken up residence."

"Critters?" Barry frowned anxiously.

Grandpa shrugged. "Nothing to worry about. None of 'em will be as big as you are. But the place is pretty stuffed with clutter, and with the daylight beginning to fade, you won't be able to see well till you hit the fluorescents. You remember where the switch is, right?"

"Is there a chain that drops down from the fixture?" Mark asked.

"Right. It's in the middle of the room," Grandpa said. "So you have to go inside before you can turn the lights on. What I was going to say was, try not to trip over anything."

Their energy restored, the three boys were out the door before Grandpa had finished speaking.

"We'll be careful," Scott called back.

"We promise," said Mark.

CHAPTER 18

The sun was low in the sky as Mark, Scott, and Barry jogged down the path toward the big red barn. The twins could hardly believe they were being allowed inside without Grandpa coming along to supervise. Did he think they were growing up, getting more mature?

Or maybe he was just counting on Barry the brainiac to be a good influence.

Grandpa Joe was what his daughter—the twins' mom—called a pack rat. He could never resist acquiring anything that might be useful even if no one else could imagine how, and he could never throw anything away. The people who used to own the property had built the red barn for horses, but Grandpa had always used it to store stuff.

The barn's front doors were huge, to accommodate horses, but the back door was a regular human size.

When Mark turned the knob and pushed it open, the hinges squealed. Inside, the air smelled like sour dust and it was hard to see after having been in daylight outdoors. A few beams of early evening light shone through chinks in the siding, but instead of lessening the gloom, they added to the creepiness.

"What kind of critters, I wonder?" Barry said as they made their way carefully across the wood floor, expecting at any moment to trip or bruise their shins.

"Mice, I guess, or bugs," Scott said.

"Or rats or spiders or *werewolves!*" said Mark, and at that very moment there was a rattling sort of flutter high above, near the far-off ceiling, and an instant later a disturbance in the air announced something was swooping in the shadows above them.

Make that some *things*—lots of them—that were squeaking as they flew.

"Bats!" shouted Barry.

"*Vampire* bats!" said Mark.

Both boys ducked and covered their heads. Scott, meanwhile, waved his arms to drive them away. "I don't even think vampire bats are for real," he said.

"Real or not, are they gone?" Barry peeked out from behind his hands.

"I don't hear them anymore, at least," said Scott. "Come on. The chain for the light's around here someplace."

A moment later, Scott's hand brushed the chain; then there was a click and a stuttering flash as the fluorescent tubing lit, casting a greenish glow over a large expanse in the middle of the room while leaving the edges and corners in shadow. With the bats and the darkness, the barn had seemed haunted. Now the harsh light and electric hum made it seem more like a mad scientist's laboratory.

But at least the boys could see. And what they saw *was* inspirational. In the well-lit center of the space were three workbenches stocked with tools, and several rows of shelving units, some stacked with paint and solvents but most with bins full of parts from every kind of machine.

In the shadows lay old and broken machines themselves—stuff anybody else would have called junk but that Grandpa called unexploited treasure. These included appliances, lawn mowers, and air conditioners.

"Is there a kitchen sink?" Barry asked after he'd had a chance to look around.

"Of course!" Mark pointed to a white porcelain fixture lying upside down, its silver pipes exposed.

"If we can't build a spaceship out of all this stuff, then we can't build one at all," Scott said.

"All this stuff . . . and Howard's computer," said Barry. "We will need a lot of computing power to plot the route and do the flying."

"The astronaut does the flying," said Mark. "Doesn't he?"

Scott said, "Or *she*," but only to annoy his brother.

Mark ignored this, and Barry said, "Not really. The astronaut has to override the computer if something goes wrong, but the computer autopilot is programmed to handle the navigation and, responding to sensors in the gyroscope, to keep the capsule stable."

The boys were all set to do some more exploring when Grandpa showed up in the doorway. By now the sky outside was dark silver, and stars twinkled behind his black silhouette. It was getting late.

"Dinner is served," he announced.

"I can't wait to call Egg," said Mark.

"And Howard," said Barry.

Scott sighed. "I guess there's no getting around Howard," he said. "We have to have that computer, not to mention what he knows about it."

"Tomorrow we meet right here," said Mark. "And we start building!"

CHAPTER 19

Only it turned out they weren't as well prepared as they first thought.

Even with all the resources in Grandpa's workshop, there was still material they needed, most important the very first thing the twins had put on their list: metal. What they were hoping for was lightweight titanium for the interior and heat-resistant nickel alloy for the outer shell. Those were the materials NASA had used for the Mercury capsules.

"Maybe we should start with the interior instead," Egg suggested. It was the following morning, and she was on the telephone with Mark. "Like, we need an instrument panel and a seat and seat belts, too. With no seat belt, the astronauts will float away."

Mark noticed she'd said "astronauts," plural. Unlike the twins, she seemed to think everyone who wanted to could still get a ride on the spaceship. Mark didn't want to argue. It was better if all of them were eager to work, and maybe they wouldn't be so eager if they realized *he* was the only one who would get to go up in space.

"Grandpa probably has an old tractor seat, but no seat belts and nothing like an instrument panel," he said.

"What about if we use a dashboard from a car?" Egg said. "Oh—and we can use a speedometer, too. In a car it measures speed by how fast the axle is rotating. Spacecraft don't have axles, but maybe there's a way to hook the speedometer to the guidance system to get the data, then recalibrate the numbers."

Mark mouthed the word "recalibrate," then tilted his head so Barry would know it was a question. Barry answered in a whisper, "It means to adjust to a different kind of measurement."

Mark nodded, then said into the phone, "Sounds good, Egg. But where do we get those things?"

"Don't you worry," Egg said. "I have an idea. Howard and I will see you this afternoon."

Grandpa had been right about the state of the workshop, and the boys spent the morning cleaning. "This is not exactly what I pictured when we thought up the idea of building a spaceship," said Mark, who was high on a ladder, knocking down cobwebs with a broom.

Scott, kneeling to corral dust and other crud in a dustpan, protested. "*Hey!* Watch where you knock down those spiders, wouldja? I think I've got a creepy-crawly in my hair!"

"Maybe he'll comb it for you, for once," Mark said.

"Look out below!" Barry cried, jumping from the top of the stepladder he'd been using to dust shelves. A moment later the hinges on the human-size barn door squealed and a girl's voice called, "Hello-o-o-o?" Then, "Yikes, it's like *magical* in here!"

"Do you think so?" Scott looked around. It was definitely a lot cleaner than it had been the previous evening, and the sunbeams that filtered through the walls seemed more jolly than eerie. Also, the bats were gone, or possibly asleep and out of sight.

"Come and help us unload," Egg said.

Parked outside was a blue commercial truck labeled NANDO'S AUTO REPAIR. A man was handing a car's old bench seat to Howard, who didn't look so sure about receiving it. Mark hurried to help him.

It was another hot day, and the man wiped sweat from his brow, then stood up straight and grinned. Egg opened her mouth to make introductions, but he spoke first. "I am Nando Perez, owner of Nando's Auto Repair. And you are?"

Mark, Scott, and Barry introduced themselves. "This is really nice of you," Mark said.

"*De nada*—don't mention it," said Nando. "My company is one of the sponsors of the science fair. This looks like a very ambitious project! I can't wait to find out what it is you're building."

Now the truck's passenger door opened, and Lisa, the girl they had seen yesterday, jumped out.

"Meet Lisa, everybody," Egg said. "She's going to help us, too."

Scott and Mark looked at one another, both thinking the same thing: Who said it was okay for Egg to invite another kid? But they didn't want to be rude to Lisa, who looked like she was kind of shy anyway, so they smiled and said "Hi."

One benefit of having a lot of helpers was that it didn't take long to unload the truck.

"Thanks, Mr. Perez," Egg said when they were done.

"What else do you need?" he asked.

"Sheet metal," she said, "if it's not too much trouble."

"I'll see what the junkyard has available," said Nando.

"We really appreciate it," Egg said. "But how do we pay you back?"

"With a blue ribbon from the science fair," Mr. Perez said.

Egg grinned. "That is a deal."

* * *

Mark and Scott were showing the other kids around the workshop when Grandpa came out to see if anybody wanted lunch.

"*Me!*" Barry, Scott, and Mark chorused.

"Whoa, Nellie!" Grandpa looked around. "You boys have sure done some good work on the cleanup."

"You're telling us," said Mark.

"Thank you," said Barry.

"And now we're going to organize our workspace," said Egg.

"Oh, goody," said Mark.

Howard looked at Mark. "That was sarcasm, right?"

"Howard, my boy." Mark clapped him on the back. "You are catching on."

"She means we organize our workspace *after* we eat lunch," said Scott. "Grandpa Joe? It's not more peanut butter and peppers, is it? I would never whine, you know that, but . . ."

Grandpa laughed. "I've got cold cuts today. And lemonade. And there might be some cookies in the cupboard."

The kids ate outside. Scott counted, and Lisa said exactly eleven words: "It's nice to meet you, Mr. McAvoy" and "Thank you, Mr. McAvoy." If she was going to be part of this group, he thought, she was going to have to learn to speak up a little. In comparison, Howard was downright chatty when you got him on the subject of computers and math.

"I've been working on the control program, but I still have a lot of math to learn about orbital mechanics," Howard said. "One thing I realized is that we'll save fuel if we launch directly to the east. Earth rotates eastward at roughly 1,000 mph, which means that effectively, the spaceship on the launchpad is traveling that fast, too."

"And so are we, for that matter," said Barry.

Howard thought for a moment and nodded. "Yes, I suppose that's true."

"Weird," said Mark.

"Anyway, that is effectively 1,000 mph worth of fuel we don't have to use. Saving fuel saves weight, which in turn saves fuel. . . ."

"The rocket equation," said Jenny. And then she said something both Mark and Scott found incomprehensible: "Change in velocity equals exhaust velocity times the natural logarithm of the initial mass divided by the final mass."

Scott looked at his brother, and his brother said, *"What?"*

"Maybe it would help if I wrote it down," Jenny said. She pulled a pencil from her pocket and wrote on the back of a napkin: $\Delta v = v_e \ln \dfrac{m_0}{m_1}$

"Oh yeah." Mark nodded sagely. "Sure. Now I get it. Perfectly clear."

"Why didn't you just say that before?" Scott asked.

"Sarcasm again?" Howard said. "Because she did say that before. The change in velocity equals the—"

Mark held up his hand. "Really, Howard. Repeating it won't help. What are you math nerds talking about?"

Jenny's and Howard's expressions said: *It's so totally obvious, there is no other way to explain it.* But Barry raised his hand. "I can give it a try. A Russian math teacher developed this equation. It describes the rocket's velocity as the fuel burns up and shrinks its mass. His name was Tsiolkovsky—Zy-ol-*koff*-skee."

"Oh!" said Scott. "So it's in Russian? No wonder we don't understand."

Mark rolled his eyes. "Math is a universal language, dummy. Uh . . . , isn't that right, Barry?"

"More or less," said Barry. "Now shut up—excuse me, *be quiet*—and I will explain. So you guys get velocity, right? It's the speed of something in a particular direction. And that little triangle is a delta sign, which means change. So the left half of the equation is change in velocity. Are you with me so far?"

Scott and Mark nodded.

"So the other half of the equation is the exhaust velocity—in other words, how fast the exhaust is spewing out of the rocket's nozzle. You multiply that times the initial mass of the rocket, which includes the fuel in the rocket, and then divide it by the final mass of the rocket, which is what's left after the fuel has burned off. Then that number gets multiplied by the natural log function, and it equals the change in velocity—the left part of the equation."

A lightbulb flashed in Mark's brain. The bulb was only about as big as a firefly, but it was definitely switched on. "So the rocket flies, and as it flies, its mass shrinks because part of its mass was fuel that has burned off in the exhaust?" Mark said. "And as the mass gets smaller, there is less fuel available but, at the same time, it takes less fuel to propel it. Is that right?"

"Yes!" said Barry.

"But what's this natural log business? It sounds like it has something to do with a fireplace," Scott asked.

"In this case it's a constant to describe something that changes continuously over time," Barry said. "So the mass of the fuel is changing and affecting the velocity not just moment by moment, but also all the moments in between. The natural log is a mathematical way to describe that."

Mark sighed. "If you say so."

"It's Tsiolkovsky who said so," said Egg.

"In Russian," Scott reminded them. "But why do you want to know this again?"

"It tells you most of what you need to know to put

a rocket in space," Egg said. "How much fuel you need, how massive your rocket and your capsule can be, and how fast you can go. It's pretty cool."

By this time lunch was over, the last lemonade drop drunk and cookie crumb devoured. Grandpa Joe had listened for a while but then gone back into the house to work on today's remodeling project, a new tile floor in the bathroom. After clearing their dishes and washing up, the kids headed back to the workshop.

CHAPTER 20

Egg's idea was that they make an inventory—a list—of all the items in the workshop, then cross-reference it with what they thought they would need. At that point, they could go back to Nando and see what additional supplies he might be able to provide.

"We also need to inventory our skill set," Egg said.

Mark looked at the other kids one by one, then asked, "Does everybody else understand her all the time?"

Egg rolled her eyes. "All I mean is, we figure out what each of us knows how to do so we know what help we'll have to ask for. Like, Howard can program a computer. But besides that there's going to be metal fabrication, and soldering, and wiring, and plumbing . . . and on and on."

"I can weld," said Lisa.

"You can?" Scott said. "Can you teach us?"

Lisa looked at her toes and nodded.

"That is so cool!" said Mark. "How does welding work, exactly?"

Lisa thought for a second. "Basically, you're using an arc of electricity to melt metal and make glue out of it. Then the glue sticks two pieces of metal together."

"Is it hard?" Egg asked.

"It's hard to do neatly," said Lisa. "You have to practice a lot."

"Okay, welding, *check*," said Egg.

"Can I ask a question?" Lisa said.

"Sure," said Mark.

"So is the secret science fair project a spacecraft?"

Everyone laughed—even Howard. Lisa turned pink, and Egg said, "Sorry, Lisa. I guess no one officially told you that yet, huh?"

Lisa shook her head.

Egg explained, "It's really only a secret from the grown-ups. We don't want them to tell us we're crazy or we can't do it. Do you think we're crazy?"

Lisa shrugged. "Not necessarily. And I won't tell. I'm good at keeping secrets."

"Unlike some people," Scott said.

"One thing, though," Lisa said. "I don't have to be an astronaut if I help out, do I? I'm claustrophobic—I don't like squished places."

"You absolutely don't have to be an astronaut," said

Scott. "There's only room for one anyway."

Egg looked up. "Oh?"

"I want to go," said Howard.

And Barry said, "Who made the decree that there's only room for one?"

"Oh, come on, you guys," said Mark. "*You're* the ones who understand the rocket equation. We're going to have a hard enough time building and fueling a small spacecraft, let alone one that holds everybody."

Egg said, "You have a point, and we should probably pick according to weight. If Lisa doesn't want to go, I'm definitely lightest."

"But it was Scott's and my idea!" said Mark.

"I didn't mean to cause a fight," Lisa said quietly.

"It's not your fault. Some people are just unreasonable," said Mark.

"So anyone who doesn't agree with you is unreasonable?" Barry said.

"That's an unreasonable assertion," said Howard.

"Guys?" said Egg. "Has anybody noticed something? Now that we're arguing, we've all stopped working. At this rate we'll never get any"—she looked around, then whispered the word—"*spacecraft* built at all. Maybe we can put off this decision."

In fact, it was almost time for Mrs. O'Malley to pick up Egg, Howard, and Lisa. Mark was still annoyed, but Scott had started to feel bad. He didn't like fighting with people, especially his friends. Deep down, he wondered if maybe Egg, Barry, and Howard might be right. Maybe it wasn't fair for him and Mark to assume one of them would be the astronaut.

And there was something else, too. All the Mercury astronauts had been superstar pilots before they ever went to work for NASA. For example, John Glenn, the first American to orbit Earth, had flown more than 150 combat missions in two wars, served as a military test pilot, and won five medals.

Meanwhile, Scott and Mark had never even been passengers in a plane. Even if a computer did do most of the work, what made them think they'd be able to fly a spacecraft?

As the group walked outside to meet Mrs. O'Malley, Scott had an idea that he voiced before it was totally thought through. "What if we have a contest?"

"A contest? What are you talking about?" Mark asked.

"To determine who gets to"—he looked around to make sure no grown-up was listening—"go up in space."

Egg looked interested. "What do we have to do in our contest?" she asked.

Scott didn't answer right away, and Barry stepped in. "My brother says the closest feeling to being a pilot is the feeling you get on amusement park rides. So maybe we should have our contest at Great Adventure."

Great Adventure was a new amusement park in

Jackson, New Jersey, not far from the twins' home in West Orange. It was supposed to be almost as big and exciting as Disney World in Florida, and Scott and Mark had been begging their parents to take them.

Mark smiled for the first time in a while. "Now you're talkin'!"

Egg said, "Lisa can come too, right?"

Mark and Scott looked at one another. This was getting to be a lot of people. On the other hand, Lisa knew how to weld. They had a feeling this might come in handy. And the space program had a lot of people working for it too.

Lisa opened her mouth to say that it was okay, she didn't have to go, but Mark cut her off. "Why not?"

Scott said, "Great Adventure sounds a lot better than cleaning and inventorying. We can tell Grandpa it's educational."

"It absolutely is," said Mark. "How can he say no?"

CHAPTER 21

"Tell me again how this is part of your spaceship project," Grandpa Joe said. It was early in the morning, two days later. Grandpa had borrowed a station wagon from a neighbor, and they were driving south on I-95. Barry's brother, Tommy, had agreed to meet them at Great Adventure to spend the day, the first day they all had free. After that, he'd drive Barry and the twins back home to West Orange.

"Pilots and astronauts train in flight simulators," Scott said. "And in jets and airplanes, too, of course."

"Which is not exactly practical for us," Mark added.

"According to Tommy, amusement park rides are the next best thing," Scott said.

A few minutes later, they turned into a parking lot

as big as a town, and Grandpa steered the car into a long line being directed by smiling teenagers wearing blue baseball caps. It was only ten o'clock, not too hot yet. Grandpa had insisted that everybody get up early so they could arrive at the park when it opened. He was determined that everyone get the most out of their five-dollar entry passes.

Walking across the asphalt, the kids and Grandpa saw Tommy standing by the ticket booths, and an instant later he waved. The twins both noticed that Tommy looked better than he had last time they saw him at Barry's house. His hair was still long, but it was clean and tied back. His beard had been trimmed. His jeans and T-shirt were clean. But the biggest improvement was the smile on his face.

Well, of course he was happy. They were going to the best amusement park in the state!

"Great to see you, pipsqueak." Tommy threw an arm around his brother's shoulders. "I know Scott and Mark, but who else—?"

"I'm Joe McAvoy." Grandpa held out his hand, and the two shook. Barry introduced Lisa, Egg, and Howard.

"Egg?" Tommy looked at her.

"You can call me Jenny if you want," she said.

Just inside the gates, Grandpa peeled off. "I'm going to get myself a regular coffee and something greasy for breakfast. You kids go on and do your thing," he said. "We can meet back here under the trees for lunch."

From the Ferris wheel to the carousel to the cotton candy carts, everything about Great Adventure was shiny, new, and colorful. Under a blue summer sky, even the blades of grass and leaves on the trees looked painted and polished.

"What do we do first?" Egg asked.

"One of the roller coasters—before they get crowded," said Barry.

Tommy shook his head no. "Actually, I have a plan. And according to the plan, we do the Big Fury coaster this afternoon." When Barry frowned, Tommy added, "Part of being either a pilot or an astronaut is being patient. Let's head for the bumper cars. First one to get there gets ten points. A-a-a-and—go!"

The kids pulled out their maps, and after a moment Mark took off, followed by Barry and then everyone else. When Mark made a wrong turn at the duck pond, Scott passed him and arrived at the bumper cars first. "Ten points for me!" he crowed.

"Points." Barry shook his head. "My brother seems to be real serious about this."

"That's a good thing," Scott said.

"Yeah, you think so because you're winning," Egg said.

"It's early yet," Mark said. "I am planning to stage an amazing comeback."

"Me too," said Lisa, and the shy, quiet way she said it made everyone laugh.

"Here's the deal," Tommy explained. "Instead of trying to hit each other with the cars, the goal is to *avoid* hitting each other. Obviously, when you're a pilot or an astronaut, collisions are a very bad idea."

Neither Scott nor Mark thought this sounded like fun till Tommy told them one more thing: He was going to drive a bumper car, too, and he wasn't going to follow his own rule.

Inside the ride, Mark chose a red car and Scott blue. They were barely strapped in when a buzz of electricity signaled that the wands were charged—and they were off! Mark imagined Tommy's black car was a spacecraft and Tommy a space alien out to destroy all that was good in the solar system. Maneuvering to avoid him, he slammed into Lisa's car—*pow!*—then called out "Sorry!" and swerved to avoid Howard, whose eyes were narrowed in concentration as he aimed for the ride's outer edge.

In an instant, Mark saw Howard's strategy. Driving on the inside, you could be hit from four directions. On the outside, you could be hit only from three. It was smart, but wimpy and annoying, Mark decided, and he jerked the wheel to cut Howard off, knowing Howard would do his best to avoid hitting him.

This worked, but Tommy called: "You lost a point, Mark Kelly!"

"Wait—*why?*"

"Rudeness!"

Soon the ride was over. The idea might have been to avoid collisions, but Mark and Scott both felt plenty bumped around as they climbed out of their cars.

"Okay, here are the point totals," Tommy announced. "Everyone but Lisa was hit at least once, and Mark was hit twice, plus he lost that point for rudeness. Scott is winning with eight points, and Lisa is next with zero. Everyone else has negative numbers, Howard and Egg with minus one, Barry with minus two, and finally Mark with minus three."

"I am dominating!" said Scott.

Mark wanted to tell his brother to shut up, but resisted. Instead, he pointed out to Lisa that she was way ahead of him with her point total of zero.

Lisa looked embarrassed. "Sorry."

"Don't be," Mark said. "You're fast and you've got good eyes. You earned that zero fair and square."

"Okay, people, listen up!" Tommy said. "Our next stop is the shooting gallery. You need good vision to be a good shot or an astronaut. Also, shooting requires steady hands, which means keeping calm under pressure. Space is a hazardous environment where you have to keep calm too."

Tommy had barely finished talking when the maps

came out and the race began. This time Mark took more care and arrived first, followed by Egg, Barry, Scott, and Lisa. Once again, Howard and Tommy brought up the rear.

"Ten points for me!" Mark said.

"It would make more sense," Egg said, "if the second- and third-place people got points, too. Otherwise there's no reason to run fast once you see you can't win."

Tommy nodded. "Okay. In that case, Egg has five points and Barry gets two."

"Whoo-hoo!" Barry cried. "I'm back to zero!"

"But that's not fair!" Mark was fuming. "You're changing the rules in the middle."

Tommy shrugged. "A good leader listens to good suggestions."

The shooting galleries were Wild West–themed, with the shooters assuming the identities of silver-starred sheriffs defending townsfolk against black-hatted villains, not to mention jackrabbits, bison, flying geese, and mountain lions.

In spite of her mild-mannered personality, Lisa's steady hands and good eyes made her an excellent shot. To everyone's surprise—including her own—she won this segment of the competition, with Barry and Scott taking second and third places. When the smoke had cleared and the dust had settled, Lisa and Scott were in the lead with ten each, then Mark with seven, Barry with five, Egg with four, and Howard with minus one.

"Where to next?" Mark was determined to make up points and figured speed was his best asset.

"Drinking fountain. It's hot out here," Tommy said.

"Can't we get sodas? Grandpa gave me money," Scott said.

Tommy shook his head. "Bad for your teeth."

"Do astronauts need good teeth?" Barry asked.

Tommy nodded. "Astronauts and pilots both."

Scott spotted a drinking fountain, sprinted to it, took his turn, and asked, "Do I get points?"

"Not this time," Tommy said.

"But Egg got a point when she asked—"

Tommy gave him a look, and Scott closed his mouth. He didn't want to lose a point for arguing.

"We've got time for one more activity before lunch," Tommy said. "Ready?"

Except for Howard, the kids got out their maps and were poised to run.

"Arcade!" Tommy said.

This time, to everyone's surprise, Howard won, and Egg was second. When the others caught up, they saw that Egg had her hands on her hips and was giving Howard a lecture about cheating.

Howard did not seem upset. Instead, he looked slightly more puzzled than usual.

When Egg ran out of adjectives, it got quiet for a moment. Then, sounding frighteningly like a grown-up, she asked, "What do you have to say for yourself?"

"I didn't cheat," Howard said. "I just used different methodology."

Egg's expression threatened to start the lecture all over again, but Tommy interrupted. "What do you mean, Howard?"

"I'm not good at reading maps," Howard said. "But I know Jenny—that is, Egg—is good at it. So when she got up from the bench quickly, I followed her, and when I saw the arcade I ran ahead and beat her. It's just the luck of my having long legs, Jenny."

Tommy nodded. "Makes sense to me. In fact, for your creative solution to the problem, Howard, you get double points!"

Howard smiled. "Thank you. I believe that puts me in the lead."

Scott groaned. "He's got nineteen! He's killing us all!"

"Now, are we ready for some pinball?" Tommy asked. "You'll be seeing Newtonian motion in action, not to mention vectors."

"Uh-oh," said Scott. "Math."

"Yesss!" said Barry.

"I didn't think I liked math either till I saw I needed it to be a pilot," said Tommy. "Planes crash if you miscalculate the relationships between lift, temperature, weight, wind speed, and thrust, not to mention the length of the runway."

"I didn't know pilots had to understand all that," Scott said.

"Engineers do all they can to make flying easy on the pilot," said Tommy. "But the pilot still has to understand the science and math. How do you think test pilots spend most of their time?"

"Hot-rodding around in fast jets," Mark said.

Tommy smiled. "That's a small part of it compared to analyzing the flying characteristics of the plane. Every flight yields hundreds of measurements, and it's up to the pilot—among others—to assess them. In fact, test pilots are constantly looking at data and trying to deduce something that will help the engineers make the airplane better."

"You mean test pilots have homework?" Scott said.

"That's just what I mean," said Tommy.

Mark and Scott were disgusted. It was bad enough that smart kids got good grades and the admiration of grown-ups. If they also got great jobs like astronaut and test pilot, then maybe the two of them should start working harder in school?

There was time to think about that one. It was still summer, after all.

The arcade was dim and cavelike, not so popular on a beautiful day. There were plenty of pinball machines to go around, and Tommy organized the kids into a tournament.

The merry mechanized music and flashing lights improved everyone's mood—especially Scott's and Mark's, because they were good at pinball. At the end of the first game, Mark, Scott, and Lisa were victorious. Since Mark and Scott had the high point totals, they each played Lisa, setting up the championship match between Mark and Scott.

"Pinball is good for two things," Tommy explained. "First, it's a way to gauge reaction times, and you have to react quickly in a spacecraft. Second, a good pinball player has to have solid hand-eye coordination, and so does a pilot."

Pinball turned out to be fun to watch, and there was a lot of fist pumping, yelling, and excitement. The last game went on for a long time, though, and Barry and Howard wandered away to check out a new kind of game played on a screen like a TV's. In it, you used lines that acted like Ping-Pong paddles to bat a white dot back and forth. It wasn't as interesting as pinball, but Barry and Howard still liked it. What could possibly be better, after all? The combination of a game *and* TV!

By the time they returned, Mark was clasping his hands over his head like a boxing champ, and the Beatles' "When I'm Sixty-Four" was playing. Scott scowled. He hated to lose—especially to his brother. Anyway, it was a dumb game—just luck and buttons.

Now it was time for lunch, and the kids made their way back to Main Street, where they were supposed to meet Grandpa. Only when they got to the benches under the trees, Grandpa was nowhere to be found. . . .

CHAPTER 22

"Isn't this where he said he'd be?" Mark looked around at the benches beneath the shade trees at the end of Main Street.

"I have an idea," said Tommy. "Let's make finding Mr. McAvoy part of the game. Whoever does gets a point— whether it's for an individual or a group. Meet back here"—he looked at his watch—"in twenty minutes, at one o'clock."

"Come on, Howard," Egg said. "You're with me."

"What?" Howard said. "Oh. All right."

Mark heard his stomach growl. All the kids had spent the morning running around with nothing to eat, and only the occasional stop at a water fountain. He was hot and tired and hungry.

Scott said to Mark, "Since he's our grandpa, let's stick together."

"Deal," said Mark. Together they took off at a jog, determined to cover maximum territory no matter how hot and sweaty they were. From Main Street to the Ferris wheel to the carousel they ran, dodging teetering toddlers. Twice they thought they saw him, once in line for lemonade and once at a hamburger stand, but both times it turned out to be only a grandpa look-alike.

No luck. Twenty minutes more exhausted, hungry, sweaty, and thirsty than before, they were back at the rendezvous, where they were astonished to find Grandpa there already.

From the smug expressions on Egg's and Howard's faces, the twins could tell they must have been the ones who found him.

Scott and Mark were glad to see their grandfather, but equally mad that they hadn't gotten the points.

"Where were you?" Mark asked.

"How did you find him?" Scott asked Egg and Howard.

"I'm fine; thanks for asking," Grandpa said.

"Sorry, Grandpa," Scott and Mark chorused.

"I got a bit warm outside and went into the soda fountain." Grandpa pointed.

"And we found him by asking people if they'd seen anyone matching Mr. McAvoy's description," said Egg.

"An old man wearing a hat," Howard clarified.

"Thanks a lot!" said Grandpa, and Egg said at the same time, *"Howard!"* Then she added, "An old *handsome* man, Mr. McAvoy."

Asking for help had never occurred to either Scott or Mark. And surely they couldn't get points for that, right? An astronaut was all alone in space.

"Egg and Howard get ten points each," said Tommy. "So now the scores are—"

"No fair!" Barry protested.

"Why not?" Lisa asked in her quiet way.

"Whose side are you on?" Barry asked. He and Lisa had worked together to find—or more accurately, not find—Mr. McAvoy.

Lisa raised one shoulder. "It was just a question."

Mark said, "We were wondering, too. Don't astronauts have to be independent and work on their own?"

"Being independent doesn't mean not asking for help," said Tommy. "All the astronauts have had Mission Control—a huge team of people—helping them when they were up in space. At one time or another, on every mission, they have needed the help from the ground. Look at Apollo 13. It was Mission Control that figured out what went wrong with the oxygen in the command module so that the three astronauts didn't suffocate or become stranded in space."

Tommy then announced the new point totals. Pinball

had given Mark and Scott a big boost, so that Mark was in the lead with thirty-seven, then Scott with thirty. After that came Howard with twenty-nine, Lisa with twenty, Egg with nineteen, and finally Barry with seven.

"How many more points can we earn, anyway?" Barry asked.

"Uh, not sure," said Tommy. "Why?"

"I want to know if there's any chance of my staging an amazing comeback, or whether I should just surrender," Barry said.

"Time for lunch?" Mark asked Grandpa.

"Up to Tommy," said Grandpa, "our fearless leader."

"First Big Fury, then lunch," said Tommy. "Think about it. Do you really want to ride a roller coaster on a full stomach?" He bent from the waist and mimed retching. *"Bleeeah!"*

"But I'm starving," said Barry.

"Me too," said Mark.

"That's a negative point for each of you," said Tommy. "Come on." He headed for the Fury, tall and purple in the distance.

"Is he just making this up as he goes along?" Egg whispered to Scott as they walked.

"Maybe," Scott said. "But we can't ask him. We'll lose more points!"

While they waited in the long line for Big Fury, Tommy gave them a lecture about the virtues of patience.

"But aren't you even hungry?" Barry asked his brother.

Tommy shrugged. "I've been through enough discomfort that a late lunch doesn't bother me."

That reminder of what Tommy had endured in the war made Mark and Scott look at each other. Then something occurred to Scott. Maybe Tommy was trying to toughen them up with this game? Not just find out who had skills and physical prowess, but mental toughness, too? Maybe he was even trying to improve their mental toughness.

"The change in G-forces on the roller coaster are like the change in G-forces when you're accelerating in a fighter plane," Tommy explained.

"G stands for 'gravitational,'" Mark said. "So G-forces measure how heavy you feel. One G means you're as heavy as you are here on Planet Earth."

"Technically, a G is the gravitational acceleration of an object near Earth's surface, if the object were in a vacuum," Barry said. "One G is right around 32 feet per second per second. But your body feels the force as weight, so that's where the idea of gravity comes in."

Tommy nodded. "When you're accelerating up the hill on a roller coaster, you feel heavier than you are, and when you go down, it's like you're lighter. That's why sometimes you feel like your stomach's lurching around inside you."

By the time Mark and Scott had snaked their way

to the front of the line, they were so excited they had forgotten about lunch. Mark looked at Egg. Was she nervous? What about Lisa? Or were they like Mom—unusually tough for girls? Barry was solid, Mark knew, if a little lazy. And Howard . . . ? He was a mystery. The normal things that might make anyone nervous didn't seem to faze him. His usual state of mind, Mark was learning, might be described as confused curiosity.

Just as they were ready to make the final turn toward the loading area, Tommy said, "Know what, guys? Change of plan. I think we should eat lunch first."

At first Mark didn't even hear him. His attention was focused on the last car disappearing over the crest of the hill at the top of the track. Then the words sank in, and he didn't believe them. Barry spoke up: "That's bogus, Tommy!"

"No fair," said Egg.

Howard looked more confused than usual; Lisa looked disappointed.

Scott was angry and about to say so when he felt a glimmer of suspicion. What was it Tommy had said earlier about being patient? About how astronauts and pilots have to roll with punches and changes of plans? The engineering of rockets and spacecraft was still new. Things went wrong all the time, sometimes tragically. Many liftoffs had been delayed and the astronauts had

had to come back the next day—or later—and try again.

So now . . . was Tommy messing with them to see how they handled disappointment?

"Come on, guys, step out of the line," Tommy said.

Barry put his foot down. "Not gonna happen, big bro."

Mark said, "It's a test, isn't it?"

"Whaddaya mean?" Tommy was obviously suppressing a grin.

Mark explained his theory, which was the same as Scott's.

"You guys might be giving me way too much credit for brainpower here," Tommy said. "But do I take it I'm wrong and you don't want to eat first? You're ready for Big Fury?"

"Yeah, we are!" said Mark.

"Okay, then. Apologies all around. Go ahead and keep your places in line. I'll catch up to you at the end."

"You don't want to ride?" Lisa asked.

Tommy shook his head and said flying in a war had provided enough thrills for one lifetime.

"Oh—but one more thing," he called out to them as they were about to climb onto the ride. "Raise your hands over your heads."

"What!?" said Howard.

"I don't even *want* to be an astronaut," Lisa protested.

Tommy grinned and raised his own hands to demonstrate. "Hands up, everybody! Anybody who gets scared and has to hold on loses a point!"

Two minutes later, Scott and Mark were being secured into their car. Their hands were up and they were grinning like maniacs. The machinery groaned as the car made the long ascent at the start of the ride. Excited as he was, Mark remembered that a roller coaster operates on kinetic energy. The car being tugged upward built up potential energy that was released on the long, fast descent.

Moments later, the kids experienced the laws of motion with gut-churning intensity. In response, Mark and Scott yelled; Egg and Barry screamed; Howard smiled; Lisa closed her eyes.

The ride was only ninety seconds long. Scott and Mark managed to keep their hands up, but everyone else had grabbed onto the car's railing at one time or another. Scott, like Egg, Howard, Barry, and Lisa, looked wobbly and a little green as he alighted. Mark was the only one with a big grin on his face. In fact, he would happily have done the ride again if only a line of people weren't waiting for his place.

Tommy took one look and said, "That clinches it."

Scott said, "What does?"

"Mark already had the most points—thirty-six. And

he was the one who recognized my scheme to test your ability to roll with the unexpected. Now he's the only one of you that doesn't look nauseated." Tommy shrugged. "With enough training, I think any of you would make a good astronaut. But if you want the best astronaut right now, it's Mark Kelly."

CHAPTER 23

Just before six o'clock at the Great Adventure main gate, the group going home to Greenwood Lake—Grandpa, Lisa, Egg, and Howard—said their good-byes to those going back to West Orange.

Lisa pulled Scott aside. "Are you going to be all right?" she asked quietly.

Scott had thought he was doing a good job of hiding his disappointment, but the anxious expression on Lisa's face told him he'd failed at that, too.

"Yeah, sure," he told her. "That spacecraft we're building looks pretty uncomfortable, actually. I mean, to keep weight down, we're not even going to pad the seat, right?"

Lisa giggled. "Okay, good. I wouldn't want to orbit Earth sitting on a rock either. See you soon. We still have a lot of work to do."

"Yeah, see you soon," Scott said.

The drive back to West Orange wasn't long. On the way, Tommy took Barry, Scott, and Mark out for burgers. They got home at nine o'clock.

All evening, Scott tried hard to be a good sport, but in truth he felt crushed. Mark might like to tease him about being dropped on his head, but in fact they were about the same amount smart and the same amount strong. Mark knew this too—didn't he? Heck, most of the time their grades were even the same, meaning equally not-that-great.

But there were times when Scott felt like Mark always edged him out, just barely. And today it wasn't only Little League or a bike race, it was something important.

What he had said to Lisa was mostly to make her feel better. Scott didn't really care that the seat was hard or that the capsule was dinky or even that the astronaut might be in deadly danger. He had really wanted to be the first kid launched into orbit. And now he wouldn't be.

Back at home, Mark was so keyed up he couldn't stop talking about pinball, the Big Fury, bumper cars, losing Grandpa, and how Tommy had turned everything into a contest.

"So who won?" Dad asked.

"Me!" Mark said.

"Ah." Mom looked at Scott. "I thought you were quieter than usual."

"I'm fine," Scott insisted.

Mom looked at Dad, and said, "Mmm-hmm."

"I'm *fine*," Scott repeated.

The family was in the living room—parents on the sofa, each boy sprawled in an easy chair. *The Mary Tyler Moore Show* was on the television with the sound turned down. Scott wished they were watching *I Dream of Jeannie*, which at least was about an astronaut, or *Gilligan's Island*, which was about people lost on a desert island. It was his favorite show and his favorite character was the Professor.

"Tommy said it wasn't really the points in the contest that mattered," Mark explained. "It was more like he wanted to see how well we reacted to changing circumstances. And we all showed we could do it—be flexible and mentally tough, I mean."

"Except Mark did it a little better than everybody else," Scott couldn't help adding. "Plus he didn't look ready to throw up after the roller coaster."

Mark shrugged. "Hey, what can I say? I'm a superior being."

Mom shot Mark a look, and he said, "Only kidding," but kept right on grinning.

"Sounds like Tommy put you through basic training, only without the backpacks and push-ups," Mr. Kelly said.

"Did you know astronauts do survival training?" Mark

asked. "Tommy told us. They spend days in the jungle and the desert in case their spacecraft are forced to land far away from the target."

"Why all this sudden interest in astronauts?" their mom asked.

"Yeah, Mark, why?" Scott asked, trying to look innocent.

That, at least made his perfect brother stammer. "Uh . . . Tommy mentioned it, uh . . . for no reason in particular, I guess. Because he's a pilot?"

If their parents noticed that Mark was flustered, they didn't say anything. "Do you remember when you were little and wanted to be astronauts?" their mom asked. "You still can be, you know. I don't think a couple of Cs in fifth grade will count too much against you—provided you work harder in the future."

Mark said, "I will, Mom."

Scott didn't say anything.

CHAPTER 24

The next morning, Mark opened his eyes and announced, "There's only a few weeks till school starts. I think we need to make a schedule or we won't get done in time for the science fair."

Scott had been awake, staring at the ceiling, for several minutes by then. "Get what done?" he asked.

"Project Blastoff—what did you think?" Mark rolled over and looked at his brother.

"Oh, that," Scott said.

"Look," Mark said, "we always knew only one of us could go. If it was the other way around, I wouldn't mind. I'd be happy for you."

Scott tilted his head to look at his brother. "Ha!"

"I would!" Mark said. "Anyway, I'd try. So you have to try too. Besides, it's not like you can quit or anything."

"Who says I can't quit?" Scott asked. "What do I care if Egg gets a blue ribbon? Maybe the grown-ups are right and we'll make a mistake and blow something up. Maybe I think Project Blastoff is dumb. Maybe I think it'll never work."

Neither twin said anything for a few moments; then Mark asked, "Do you think that?"

"Yes," Scott said. "No. I don't know. I'm just mad, I guess. And disappointed. And life is unfair, and I wish I didn't have a brother, and I don't even like you, and I'm hungry."

"Well, I don't like you either," said Mark. "Do you want pancakes for breakfast? I'll make 'em."

Scott wasn't sure how pancakes were supposed to make up for his not getting to go into space, but he knew that was what Mark meant by the offer.

"I think I'd rather not be poisoned, thank you."

"Funny, very funny." Mark climbed out of bed and started to get dressed. "Did you know vomit in space is even more disgusting than vomit on Earth? It floats around in blobs and you have to chase it and catch it because if it hits the wall or your spacesuit, it'll smear and get everywhere."

"Thank you for telling me that before breakfast," Scott said.

"You're welcome. Plus if you vomit with your space helmet on, you can drown in it. I mean, for real, drown in your own vomit. I found out something about going to the bathroom if you stay in space a long time, too. Since there's no gravity, you have to attach a vacuum system to—"

"Ewww!" Scott said. "Can we change the subject?" Then he threw off his covers, climbed out of bed, and left the bedroom, heading for the bathroom. While in there, he silently thanked nature for providing gravity, which made so many things easier.

CHAPTER 25

Luckily for Scott's digestion, Dad, who had the day off, was already in the kitchen mixing up batter when the two boys made their appearance.

"What have you got going on today?" Dad asked them.

"Is there a calendar around?" Mark answered the question with a question. "We need to make a schedule so we can get our project done."

"My gosh, you guys *are* serious. Sure—there's a calendar on the desk in the den. You can get it after breakfast." Dad served their plates.

Mom, who was off too, came in and sat down at the table. "Did somebody say schedule?" she asked. "I can fill in items one and two—weeding and mowing."

The twins groaned because they knew they were

expected to groan, but really their mom's request made them both realize something important. If they were going to convince their parents to take them to Greenwood Lake a whole bunch of times in the next few months, they would have to be model members of the household.

No taking apart calculators or other valuable devices. No "forgetting" to walk Major Nelson. No leaving their bicycles in the driveway instead of the garage. No talking back. In fact, they would probably have to volunteer to do extra chores.

It was going to be horrible.

But if the launch from Greenwood Lake was success-ful, it would all be worth it.

If the launch was successful?

Make that *when* the launch was successful!

Breakfast over, Mark and Scott both jumped up to clear the table and do the dishes.

"You just relax, Mom and Dad," Mark said. "Did we mention those pancakes were delicious, by the way?"

"How about another cup of coffee?" Scott offered.

Dad raised his eyebrows and looked at Mom, who said, "They're up to something."

Dad nodded. "That's for sure, but let's enjoy it while it lasts."

Once the kitchen was clean, the boys settled down

to write their schedule. As they wrote, they realized that Howard, Lisa, and Egg were going to have to do a lot of the work without them. Meanwhile, as model citizens, the twins hoped they could convince Mom and Dad to let them stay at Grandpa's as much as possible.

The schedule took a while to complete, and when it was done it looked like this:

Week of Aug. 3, 1975: Add instruments to instrument panel; complete cockpit console, including wiring and communications equipment. Begin constructing heat shield.

Week of Aug. 10: Begin capsule construction; build periscope. Begin construction of launch site bunker and launch pad.

Week of Aug. 17: Integrate seat and instrument panel and console to capsule. Install flight computer. Connect all wiring. Install attitude controller, periscope, window, and communications antenna to outside of capsule.

Week of Aug. 24: Complete launch site bunker. Install parachutes and attitude control jets. Install heat shield.

Week of Aug. 31: Begin constructing launch vehicle (rocket), rocket engine, and fuel tank. Integrate environmental system including air and water tanks to capsule. Complete construction of launch pad.

Week of Sept. 7: Move construction operations to launch site. (School starts in West Milford.)

Week of Sept. 14: Integrate fuel tank and rocket engine to the launch vehicle. (School starts in West Orange.)

Week of Sept. 21: Integrate spacecraft to launch vehicle at the launch pad.

Weeks of Sept. 28–Oct. 19: Testing of spacecraft and rocket systems. Simulations of mission, including a full dry run of launch day and launch countdown.

Oct. 24: Raise rocket with capsule into the launch position on the pad. Fuel the rocket and pressurize the tanks.

Oct. 25: L-0. Also known as . . . Launch Day!

"Now all you have to do is recopy it to send to Egg," Mark said.

"So while I'm wearing my fingers to the bone making this copy, what useful thing are *you* going to do?" Scott asked.

"Ride my bike," Mark said, and when he saw his brother scowl, he added, "Maybe some push-ups. I've gotta get in shape if I'm gonna be an astronaut. All those guys are really strong."

"How about if you get in shape by mowing the lawn?" Scott said. "I'll be out there in the hot sun to help just as soon as I finish working on this. Don't be surprised if it takes me a long time to finish up with it, though."

CHAPTER 26

An engineer named Max Faget designed the original Mercury space capsule for NASA. It had to withstand being launched on top of a rocket, orbiting Earth, and falling back through the atmosphere while also protecting anything and anyone inside. The capsule looked like an upside-down wooden top, more stubby than streamlined because it would experience air resistance only briefly during its flight.

The capsule's squat shape had another advantage as well. It would create drag to help slow the capsule down during descent.

Over the course of the next six weeks, Mark and Scott not only learned from Lisa how to weld the exterior surfaces of the spacecraft, they also learned from Grandpa how to use a shear to cut and roll sheet metal, how to plumb the pressurized environmental systems, and how to wire the electrical instruments in the cockpit.

The kids' plans were based on drawings found in books in the library, some of them surprisingly detailed, complete with dimensions and specifications for materials. The kids didn't have access to the shiny new components that NASA used and had to make do with what they had on hand at Grandpa's workshop and with what Nando could get from the wrecking yard.

For that reason, they did a lot of hammering and bending to force items to fit together. The big rubber mallet Grandpa Joe kept in his workshop came in very handy. So did the scuba tanks Grandpa had salvaged from a dive shop going out of business. The tanks would provide the air for the capsule.

Among the most important components of the spacecraft was the heat shield that covered the blunt end of the capsule. If it didn't work, the capsule would burn up on re-entry.

But how to make one?

It was Egg—who could engineer a blueberry pie—who had the idea of taking fireproof insulation from an old building, shaping it into bricks, and covering the bricks with duct tape. Grandpa got a sheet of fiberglass from a swimming pool company, and the kids affixed the bricks three deep to that sheet. For the innermost layer, they used a badly scratched oak tabletop Grandpa had purchased at a flea market years before.

"It's probably time I admit to myself that I'm never going to get around to refinishing this," he told Scott and Mark when he lent it to the cause. "But it proves my point that junk is worth keeping around."

The nylon parachutes came from a friend of Mrs. O'Malley's who used to be in the air force. Lisa could not only weld, she could sew, and she stitched them together to form the two chutes they needed.

When the police department in West Orange announced it was upgrading its radio system, the twins' parents agreed to liberate some of the old police radios before they were scrapped.

"Why is it you need radios again?" Mr. Kelly asked Mark as he handed over a cardboard box brimming with components and disconnected wires.

"For the project," Mark said simply.

"Right. The project," Mr. Kelly said. "And you're sure it's safe?"

"Dad," Mark said, "even Scott and I couldn't blow anything up using old police radios. Could we?"

"If anyone could, it's you two," Dad said.

The project taught them resourcefulness and building skills and something else, too: how to work as a team.

Different as they were, Mark, Scott, Barry, Howard, Egg, and Lisa had to get along. When there were disagreements, the twins kept in mind that each person had something to offer the group and the project. None could have built a spacecraft alone, not even with all the time in the world. Experience taught them that doing something hard requires a skill called collaboration.

It was on a Friday in late August that Mr. Perez came into Grandpa's workshop carrying a sheet of titanium he'd been lucky to find at the junkyard.

"Where do you want me to put this?" he asked Howard, who was nearest the door.

"Oh, great, thanks." Howard pointed to a section of the workshop where other metal sheets were leaning against the wall. "Do you need some help?"

"I've got it," said Mr. Perez. He dropped off the piece of metal and surveyed the work in progress. "You know," he said at last, "if I didn't know better, I'd say you're building a darned good replica of a Mercury capsule like *Friendship 7.*"

Lisa had been kneeling on the floor, soldering electrical connections in the instrument panel. Now she pulled off her work goggles, wiped the sweat from her forehead, stood up, and looked at her friends. Egg and Scott were installing a heat sensor. Mark was working on the antenna fairing. Barry was tightening a pipe fitting for the oxygen system.

"Guys," said Lisa to get their attention. "Maybe it's time we let him in on the secret."

The other kids stopped working and looked up. Taking her cue from Lisa, Egg spoke up. "Uh, sure. I guess so at this point."

Lisa said, "That's exactly what it is, Dad. A replica."

"A replica!" Egg and Scott repeated.

"Good word," said Mark.

"It's not so much a secret from you," said Egg. "Mostly, it's a secret from Steve Peluso. I'm going to enter it in the science fair, and I don't want him to find out in advance."

Mr. Perez shook his head. "No, no. I won't say anything. It's just a science fair project, after all. I mean, you don't, uh . . . have any intention of launching it, right? I don't see a rocket anywhere."

"I'm not gonna fly in it," Lisa said truthfully.

Egg looked at Mr. Perez. "You probably think we're crazy, right? To do all this work?"

"I think your ambition is admirable," said Mr. Perez, "and yes, a little bit crazy."

Mark had a brainstorm. "Crazy—that's it! We can call our spacecraft *Crazy 1*!"

The kids had been looking for a name. So far they had rejected Jersey Jet, Greenwood Hornet, Leapin' Lizard, and Kellys' Komet.

"I get it." Howard nodded. "Like, 'That Mark, he is a crazy one.'"

"Sounds wrong somehow," Barry said. "The Mercury

spacecrafts all had the number 7 for the seven original astronauts."

"So in that case, how about *Crazy 6*?" Scott suggested. "For the six of us."

"What about Grandpa? He helped," said Mark.

"And Mr. Perez," said Egg.

"Oh, you kids don't have to—" Mr. Perez began.

"No, Mr. Perez, we do have to! And anyway, that makes it better," said Egg. "The *Crazy 8*!"

"It does have a certain ring to it," said Mark.

"It does," said Howard solemnly.

"Let's put it to a vote," Egg said. "All in favor of naming our spaceship *Crazy 8*?"

"Aye!" said all six kids.

"Aye!" said Mr. Perez. "And thanks."

They had a name, an astronaut, and a launch site. Very soon they would have a spacecraft. Only one big problem remained. They needed the rocket itself—the vehicle that would launch their spacecraft into orbit. And they needed a way to fuel it.

....

CHAPTER 27

"I can't believe we're going to school a week before we have to," Mark grumbled to his brother.

It was the second Monday in September. Along with Mrs. O'Malley, the twins were climbing the steps toward the front doors of Egg, Lisa, and Howard's elementary school in West Milford. The boys were spending their last week of summer at the lake with their grandpa so they could work on the spacecraft. Egg had asked them to come by that day to meet Mr. Drizzle, her science teacher.

"A school, not *our* school," Scott reminded his brother. "It's all these poor kids who are prisoners, while we enjoy another week of freedom."

Following at a reluctant distance, the twins walked down the first-floor corridor past the school office. In spite of the number of kids who had trodden on it that day, the linoleum remained shiny and unscuffed, and everything smelled like a combination of floor polish, school cafeteria pizza, and paper fresh off the mimeograph machine.

Mr. Drizzle's room, Room 7, was at the far end of the first-floor hallway.

The door was open, and inside was a man seated at a desk. Two kids—Egg and a boy with curly brown hair—were standing before him.

The man's hair was gray and in need of combing. He had a beaky nose. He wore black pants, a short-sleeved shirt with a paisley pattern, and a blue-and-green tie. His translucently pale skin had a dusting of cinnamon-colored freckles. When the boys walked in, he nodded, but then he saw Mrs. O'Malley and stood up.

Meanwhile, Egg and the boy continued their argument at an ever-increasing volume.

"*Enough,*" the man said at last. Egg and the boy were instantly silent. "Good afternoon, Mrs. O'Malley. Jenny told me we'd have visitors. I'm Mr. Drizzle."

The twins had the same thought at the same time— they should've identified this guy immediately, based on his looks. Mr. Drizzle was the typical nutty-professor type.

"I hear you have quite a project, a secret project, for the science fair," Mr. Drizzle said. "Now, don't worry. I'm not even going to ask. Just promise me you won't—"

"—blow anything up." Mark and Scott finished his sentence for him.

"We won't," Mark added.

"It's not fair," said the scowling boy with curly brown hair.

"There's nothing in the rules, so it is too," said Egg, and it was apparent this was the subject of their argument. "Tell him it's fair, Mr. Drizzle."

"The rules are mum on the subject of collaborators, Steve," said Mr. Drizzle.

Aha—so this must be the famous Steve Peluso, defending science fair champion. Mark and Scott sized him up and came to the same conclusion: He didn't look so smart. They were pretty sure they—that is, Egg—could beat him.

Steve shot the twins an evil look. "They don't even go to our school!"

Mr. Drizzle's voice was sympathetic but firm. "The rule book doesn't mention that either. Jenny has to write her presentation and make her display, but if she wants help on the underlying project, she can have it. When you won with your mechanized model of the solar system, you were using the work of other scientists—Galileo and Kepler."

"Yeah, and your dad probably did most of the work for you anyway," Egg said.

Egg's mom frowned.

"Sorry," said Egg.

Mr. Drizzle continued. "Steve, you're welcome to recruit help yourself, if you want."

Steve did not appear to be listening. He turned and headed for the door. "You know my dad's on the school board, right?" he said as a parting shot—and then he stalked off down the hall.

Mr. Drizzle sighed. "The whole world knows Steve's dad is on the school board. At the same time, he is a very bright young man. Now"—he shook his head, changing gears—"I know your project is a secret, but Jenny did say it has something to do with outer space. If by chance that means rocketry, I might be able to help. Rocketry's been an interest of mine since I read a biography of Robert Goddard as a boy."

"Who's Robert Goddard?" asked Scott.

Egg slapped her forehead. "You know," she said. "That rocket nozzle design we were looking at last week? He invented it."

"No, he didn't," Mark corrected her. "Gustav de Laval invented it for use in steam turbines. But Robert Goddard was the first to use it for rocketry."

"So no wonder I'm confused," Scott said. "What's so special about it again? I must've been gimbaling the gyros that day."

"It's wide at the intake and the exhaust—the top and the bottom—and narrow in the middle," Mark explained.

"When the propellant goes through, it gets compressed in the middle, which makes the flow out the bottom end faster."

"Supersonic, actually," Egg said. "In other words, the nozzle makes the fuel more efficient so it provides more power."

"So I take it your project *does* have a rocket component," Mr. Drizzle said.

Egg nodded. "Look, if I tell you what it is, do you promise not to tell anyone?"

"She means Steve," said Mark.

"Are you going to tell me at long last as well?" Mrs. O'Malley asked.

The kids looked at one another. So far, the only grown-ups who knew they were building a spacecraft were Grandpa, Mr. Perez, and—if he counted as a grown-up—Tommy. They had tried to keep the whole thing a secret, but they really did need help.

"It's up to you," Mark said to Egg.

She nodded, took a breath, and told Mr. Drizzle about *Crazy 8*, leaving out one little detail—that they really did plan to launch it into space.

"We've solved a lot of problems," Egg went on. "But we still need fuel and a launch vehicle powerful enough to put our spacecraft into orbit."

"She means we *would* need to," Mark clarified, "*if* we were going to put our spacecraft into orbit."

"Right," Egg said. "But since the goal is to make the project as realistic as possible, we want to be able to show there is a rocket that would work. If possible, we'd like to build that, too."

Mark said, "In the Apollo program, NASA uses refined kerosene and liquid oxygen for stage 1 of the Saturn rocket, and liquid hydrogen and liquid oxygen for stages 2 and 3. But we could never afford as much as we would need. Not to mention, there's a safety issue."

"Because we don't want to blow anything up," Scott said.

Mr. Drizzle stood, went to the blackboard, and picked up a piece of chalk. "To understand fuels, you have to understand some chemistry. Can anybody define 'fuel' for me?"

Mark and Scott frowned. They wanted rocket fuel, not a chemistry lesson.

Mr. Drizzle seemed to read their minds and shrugged. "What can I say? I'm a teacher."

Scott kept right on frowning, but Mark's know-it-all impulse kicked in. "Uh, a fuel is something that you burn to make something else move—like gasoline in a car."

Not to be outdone, Egg added, "Or to warm something up—like wood in a fireplace."

Mr. Drizzle nodded. "The burning, or more technically the combustion, of a fuel results in rapidly expanding gases. In a car, the gases make the pistons go up and down. In a rocket, the gasses exit the nozzle, propelling the nose in the opposite direction. The idea behind a simple solid-fuel rocket is straightforward. What you want to do is create something that burns very quickly but does not explode. The fuels we're most familiar with—like methane, kerosene, and gasoline—are hydrocarbons, composed of carbon and hydrogen atoms."

"Got it," said Egg.

"Now, as it happens," Mr. Drizzle said, "there is a solution to your problem based on something with a similar chemical composition: hydrogen, carbon, and oxygen. Have you kids heard of sugar propellants? Some people call them rocket candy. Most of them aren't as powerful as what NASA's using, but they're cheaper and a lot more stable."

"Plus they probably taste better," said Mark.

Mr. Drizzle made a face. "I wouldn't volunteer for the taste test myself. But I have been experimenting with some novel ways to formulate sugar propellants, and I've designed a single-stage, solid-fuel, lightweight, optimally efficient rocket and rocket engine. Smaller than either the Redstone or the Atlas, the Drizzle rocket delivers a major upgrade in performance over competing launch vehicles."

"Whoa," said Mrs. O'Malley. "If this teaching-science gig doesn't work out for you, you could definitely go into used car sales."

"Thank you," said Mr. Drizzle.

"But what's in your solid rocket fuel, anyway?" Scott asked.

"Sugar, molasses, powdered aluminum, and bubble gum," Mr. Drizzle replied.

"Bubble gum?" Egg and the twins chorused.

"That's what binds it all together," he explained, "and then, naturally, there is a secret ingredient of my own invention, one whose chemical components I cannot yet divulge. NASA doesn't even have this one yet."

Egg looked skeptical. "How major an upgrade over existing technology are we talking about?"

"I can't be sure," said Mr. Drizzle, "because my results are based on lab experiments only. But if my calculations are correct, the specific impulse would be around 350 seconds."

Mrs. O'Malley raised her hand. "Uh, excuse me. Not to sound stupid, but—*specific impulse?*"

"It's a measure of how much power a propellant delivers in a given time," Mr. Drizzle said.

"You need a fuel capable of delivering a high specific impulse—a bunch of power in a short time—if it's going to put a spacecraft in orbit, Mom," Egg said.

"So what does a specific impulse of 350 seconds mean?" Mrs. O'Malley asked.

Egg, Mark, and Scott were smiling. With Barry's help they had already done the calculations based on the weight of their spacecraft and their astronaut. If the rocket and rocket engine were truly lightweight, they knew exactly the specific impulse they needed.

Egg answered for all of them. "It's enough to launch a 3,000-pound spacecraft into orbit, Mom—a spacecraft right about the size of *Friendship 7*."

Or the size of *Crazy 8*.

••

CHAPTER 28

That school year, Mark and Scott were assigned to the same sixth-grade class, with Mr. Hackess as their teacher.

Mr. Hackess had been teaching sixth grade for thirty years and using the same first-day-of-school assignment for twenty-five of them, an essay called "Three Things I Learned This Summer."

"Three Things I Learned This Summer"
by Mark Kelly

One thing I learned this summer is how to be an astronaut. How you do this is you practice a lot. How you practice is you have a simulator. You can make one out of boxes if you don't have a big budget. You cut up the boxes into the right shapes, then put labels on with markers and tape to show controls. Then you lie there and your brother tells you a thing that could go wrong for an astronaut, and you tell him what you would do if you were the astronaut. And you show him with the pretend controls how you would do it.

Another thing I learned is how to build a rocket. You need to learn how to fabricate with metal to do this. One of the tools you use is called a sheet roller, and another one is called a metal shear. My friend Lisa and her dad Mr. Perez helped teach me how to use them. It was hard but after a while I got the hang of it.

The third thing I learned is that NASA launched a probe to Mars in August. No rocket from Earth has ever gone there before that we know about. The mission's name is Viking. It will arrive at Mars next summer. I think it would be cool to go to Mars.

"Three Things I Learned This Summer" by Scott Kelly

I learned there is no up or down if you are in space. So you have to have an IMU in your spacecraft. IMU stands for inertial measuring unit. It has gyroscopes. When your spacecraft moves, the gyroscopes swivel around in a bracket called a gimbal to show what your spacecraft is doing in comparison to them, like whether it is rolling over or facing right or left or tilting up and down. This is called your spacecraft's *attitude*, and it is not the same as being grumpy or happy or can-do.

I learned an important thing that Albert Einstein figured out. What it is is time slows down for objects moving very fast through space. So an astronaut going very fast in space gets older a tiny bit less fast than someone going a normal speed. This is true, but from my own experience it does not make sense. Here is an example. I worked very fast for most of the summer, and time seemed to go very fast, too.

I learned my brother, Mark Kelly, is a little better at riding roller coasters than me.

When Mark and Scott got their papers back, they both had "Excellent!" written at the top in red ink. On Mark's it said "Very creative!" On Scott's it said "Nice use of vocabulary!" Mr. and Mrs. Kelly were so proud, they posted them side by side on the refrigerator.

···

CHAPTER 29

The *Crazy 8* team tried their best to stay on schedule, but still they got behind. It wasn't till a Saturday in late September that they were ready to move operations to the launch site, and Lisa asked her dad if he could lend a hand—and a truck.

"The launch site?" Mr. Perez repeated. "But you don't have a launch site."

"Actually," Scott said, "we do."

Egg jumped in to explain. "It's because we want everything to be as realistic as possible. So Scott and Mark found a launch site."

"We've been working there, too," said Mark, "building a blockhouse, uh . . . for optimum realism."

Besides the truck, a forklift and a cherry picker were

required to raise the pieces onto the trailer and secure them under tarps. Seeing all the help they were getting, Mark began to worry. "How are we ever going to be able to repay these nice people?"

"Chocolate chip cookies," said Egg. "After the launch—after the science fair—we will bake about a zillion."

The weather that fall was great—Indian summer, everybody called it. If things had been normal, Mark and Scott would have raced through their homework every day and gone outside to ride bikes. But things hadn't been normal since Grandpa had had the bright idea that they should build something together so they'd stop fighting.

So instead, what they did with every spare moment was run simulations. In fact, the simulator made from boxes had been repaired so many times, it was more duct tape than cardboard and the labels describing what was where had fallen off.

Scott told Mark it was okay about the labels—by now Mark should know every switch, control, and display so well that he didn't need them—and Mark realized it was true. He did know them. All the practice had done its job. They were going to be ready.

Then came the Tuesday afternoon before launch, and everything changed.

Mark thought back over what happened that day

approximately one zillion times. He tried to blame somebody other than himself, but in the end he couldn't. He
was too honest. Sure, he had had help from forces outside his control. But you couldn't really blame a little kid
for being a little kid, or a dog for being a dog.

"Just one more," Scott had said. He was sitting on his
bed, which in the simulation was Mission Control.

"I can't," Mark said.

"You can have a break after one more."

Mark took a deep breath, squinched his eyes closed,
let the breath out, and opened his eyes. "Okay, fine.
What went wrong this time?"

"You're in a spin."

"How fast?"

"One revolution per second. What happens?"

Mark tried to imagine spinning in zero gravity. *Crazy
8* had a single tiny window: depending on the attitude
of the spacecraft, the stars, the moon, and Earth would
appear in it and be gone at a dizzying rate.

"Uh . . . my vision blurs. I've got maybe half a minute
till I black out."

"Check. What do you do?"

"Check fuel level."

"It's 30 percent—way less than what you expect."

"Uh . . . maybe one of the reaction control system—
RCS—thrusters is stuck?"

"Maybe. What do you do?

"Curse Egg for doing a bad job building the thruster?"

"Not helpful."

"It might be a short circuit."

"It might, but you can't exactly rewire the system at this point."

"So I ask Mission Control to look at the telemetry. Maybe they can identify the broken thruster."

"You're out of radio range."

"Are you kidding me?"

"You're out of range!"

"Okay, okay, you don't have to yell. Well . . . then maybe I close the valves one by one till the bad one stops firing, then I go back and reopen the good ones."

"Maybe you do? You're about to black out!"

"Okay, definitely—that's definitely what I do." Playing the part of the thruster controls were old light switches. As Mark flipped each one, Scott made whooshing noises to signify the sound of firing thrusters. Finally, Scott was silent—and Mark knew he'd hit the right one.

"I'm safe!" Mark announced.

"Wait—now you hear a crackle on your headset, and I say: *Crazy 8,* this is Greenwood Control, do you read me?"

"Roger. Go ahead, Greenwood Control."

"The radar says you're out of attitude 15 degrees in

yaw, and your RCS fuel is low. What happened up there? Over."

"I don't know. I went into a spin and had to shut down the RCS and we wasted a lot of fuel before I could figure out which one to turn off."

"Uh-oh, *Crazy 8*. You know what that means, right? Over."

"Uh . . . I'm not spinning anymore?"

"*Besides* that."

"Uh—oh yeah. Without sufficient fuel for the RCS, I won't be able to control attitude during re-entry. I could be in a tough spot."

"That's affirmative, *Crazy 8*. Howard is going to send new re-entry targets for you to type into the computer. You will have to come home sooner and not make the complete orbit. We don't want you to run out of fuel. Looks like you'll be landing either in California or Nevada. Look for a big hole in the ground—that's the Grand Canyon. Oh—and I'll tell Mom you're going to be late for dinner."

"Roger that," said Mark. "Can we take a break now?"

"You go ahead," Scott said. "I'm just going to work on the checklist some more."

Mark didn't argue. In fact, he was grateful for his brother's hard work. The checklist was the list of what to do at each point in the mission, from prelaunch to recovery. If the flight was going to go smoothly, if Mark was going to be safe, nothing could be forgotten.

In the homemade simulator, Mark had to lie on his back with his bent legs draped over a footstool. It had been uncomfortable at first, but by now he was getting used to it. With one thing on his mind—getting out of the house—he pivoted free of the simulator seat, rocked back onto his shoulders, and kicked forward to a standing position. Then he trotted past Scott, through the bedroom doorway, down the hall and out the front door.

Mission accomplished: He was in the sunshine at last!

Mom and Dad were both at work. Major Nelson was probably napping on the sofa in the living room. He wasn't allowed to be up there, but he knew Scott and Mark didn't enforce the rules the way Mr. and Mrs. Kelly did.

Later Mark realized the dog must have woken up when he heard the door open.

Now that he was outside, Mark didn't have a clear idea of what he wanted to do. Grab his bike? Climb a tree? Chuck a ball against the garage door?

For a moment, it was good just to feel the sunshine, and he wished he were a normal kid with nothing better to do than go to school and come home and watch TV.

Out of the corner of his eye, Mark saw little Lori from next door riding her pink bicycle on the sidewalk. The training wheels were off, and she looked pretty confident. He bet her mom was watching through the kitchen window and looked over. There she was, and she waved at him. He waved back and at the same time heard a thump behind him.

It took him half a second to identify the reason for the thump and half a second more to foresee what was going to happen next—and in that time the catastrophe had already begun to play out. Major Nelson, convinced that bicycles are a constant and dangerous threat, was galloping full speed toward Lori.

"Major Nelson!" Mark yelled, and took off across the front yard.

Somewhere in the back of his mind, he saw himself as a body in motion accelerating on a vector, hoping to intersect a canine body in motion before it intersected a third body, this one on wheels and five years old.

This could all be plotted out on x and y coordinates, the velocities represented by V and acceleration by A. Howard could enter it into his computer, or Barry into his brain. Using trigonometry to solve it, you'd shortly have at least a theoretical answer to the question: Will Mark stop Major Nelson before Major Nelson knocks Lori down?

Of course, math could not answer every question— like how long Lori would cry and how mad her mother would be.

It was those unknowns that propelled Mark into a last-second Hail Mary leap that described a neat arc ending at the point on the sidewalk at which Major Nelson was tackled.

Lori, meanwhile, was surprised but unhurt.

And Mark's left arm was broken.

CHAPTER 30

"So I guess you're happy," Mark said.

It was later that same night, the lights were out, and the boys were in bed at last. With all the excitement, it was the first time they had been alone together since the accident. Mark had a cast on his arm. The doctor had given him a pill to take for pain, but Mark told his parents he didn't want it.

"No, I'm not happy," Scott said. "And that's a mean thing to say. I know you're disappointed and your arm hurts, but it's still mean, so take it back."

"I won't," said Mark.

"We can wait and launch when your arm heals," Scott said.

"Ha!" said Mark. "By the time my arm's better, the weather will be too chancy, not to mention that we can't leave the rocket sitting out that long. Somebody will see it and ask questions. Besides, Egg's Science Fair is in two weeks."

"So Barry can fly. It doesn't have to be me," Scott said.

"You're the only one who's done all the sims with me. You're flying, and I'm Mission Control, and that's the only thing that'll work. So, like I said, I guess you're happy."

"You're right," Scott said. "I am. In fact, you didn't see me, but I let Major Nelson out on purpose so he'd go after Lori and you'd have to chase him and get hurt."

There was a pause; then Mark made a sound halfway between a grunt and a chuckle. "That's what I figured," he said.

Scott started to throw a pillow at his brother but changed his mind at the last second. In the dark, he might hit the bad arm. "You could've just let Major Nelson catch Lori, you know," Scott said. "She'd have a skinned knee, probably, but so what. Her mom would've put a Big Bird Band-Aid on it and she'd be all better."

"Or maybe she'd have the broken arm," said Mark. "He's our dog. I would've felt awful. Besides, her mom was watching."

"It's like Grandpa says. No good deed goes unpunished," Scott said, and—*pow*—a pillow hit him in the face. Who knew his brother could throw so well right-handed?

* * *

The next morning the twins were awakened by a knock on their door.

"There's a young lady on the telephone for you guys," Mom said after she cracked the door open. "She's really upset about Mark's broken arm—practically in tears. I had no idea she cared that much about either one of you."

Mark had been wide-awake for a long time. "Come on. We can share the phone."

Scott rolled over and asked groggily, "What time is it?"

"Seven fifteen," said his mom. "Rise and shine!"

"I knew something was going to go wrong!" Egg moaned when the boys picked up. "Why didn't you call last night?"

"Uh, it was a little busy last night—you know, the emergency room and everything," Mark said.

"Oh gosh, I'm a horrible person. How are you feeling, Mark?" Egg asked.

"Most of me is fine," Mark said. "It's only the left arm that doesn't work so good. Anyway, Scott can fly. We've got it all worked out."

"Are you sure?" Egg asked.

"Sure, I'm sure," Mark said.

"Uh—Scott? Are you there?" Egg asked.

"Good morning, Egg," Scott said.

"Can you fly?" she asked.

"Mark says I can," Scott said. "But how did you even find out what happened? We were going to call you today."

"Your grandpa knows how important the project is to us," Egg said. "He called my mom."

The doorbell rang after breakfast. It was Barry. Over one arm he carried a plastic garment bag like the kind you get at the dry cleaning store. In his other arm was a square box big enough for a fishbowl.

"Uh-oh," Barry said when he saw Mark's arm.

"It's okay," Mark said. "Scott's going to fly." And the two of them took turns explaining what happened.

"Oka-a-a-ay," Barry said. "If you say so." But he didn't look sure.

"It's gonna be fine," Scott said. If he kept repeating it, he reasoned, he would convince himself, too. "Come in if you want." He stood aside and asked, "What's in the bag?" at the same time his brother said, "What's in the box?"

Barry held the garment bag out to Mark. "It's for you," he said; then he seemed to reconsider and pulled it back. "That is, I guess now it's for *you*." He looked at Scott. "And so is this."

"Are you sure?" Scott asked.

"Sorry. You're the same size, right? You look like you're the same size."

"We are," Scott said.

"Okay, then here. Take it—take them both." He handed the bag and the box to Scott. "Go ahead and open them."

When Scott pulled the black plastic off the hanger and saw what was underneath he was speechless, and Mark gasped.

"Okay, now I really am sorry you're going and not me," Mark said.

Under the plastic was a silver flight suit with an American flag stitched to the chest. It was a beautiful thing, even though it wasn't exactly like what the Mercury astronauts wore. Their fully pressurized suits were uncomfortable, hard to move in, and—the kids had decided—unnecessary because they didn't have the time to make one anyway.

"Where did you get it?" Scott asked.

"Tommy was some kind of spy-plane pilot. They wore these fancy suits, and he remade his for you. It's only partial pressure, but it'll give you some protection."

"More important, it looks totally cool!" Mark said.

Scott was so overwhelmed, he didn't know what to say—so he said something dumb. "I didn't know Tommy could sew."

"He can now," Barry said. "He taught himself, but I guess it wasn't easy. There are three layers of nylon, then a layer of fireproof fabric on the outside. You should have heard him yelling at the sewing machine. And there's something else, too."

He tapped the box. Now that the twins had seen what was in the plastic, they had a pretty good idea about what was in the box. And they were right: a space helmet!

"Cool!" Mark said, and with no hesitation, Scott tugged it down over his head.

Barry laughed and called out: "Hello in there! Is it a little big?"

Scott put two hands on the helmet and wiggled it. It moved, but not too much. Then apparently he spoke, but whatever he said could not be understood.

"Take it off!" Mark said. "Is there a mike in there? Speakers? I mean, I know it's a lot to ask . . . ."

"That can all be rigged up, according to Tommy," Barry said. "It's for a pilot—not an astronaut. But it'll protect your head, at least."

Meanwhile, Scott was tugging the helmet off. When at last his head was free, there was a big smile on his face.

CHAPTER 31

··

The launch was scheduled for Saturday, October 25. The night before, Friday, the twins and Barry slept in Twin Territory.

Staring out the ten-inch-high window at floor level the next morning, Mark thought he had never been so happy to see the sun rise. Lying in his sleeping bag on the mattress on the floor, Mark had been staring out for what seemed like hours, waiting for any glimmer of gray sky. At first, when the black began to fade, he thought he was imagining it, but little by little he realized his wish had been granted. At last it was getting light.

The throbbing in his arm hurt more than ever—more, even, than on the first night after the accident. He wondered if worry caused that. He had tried reminding himself that whatever happened, it would be over by noon today; that tonight, when he crawled into bed, he wouldn't have to worry about the launch anymore—wouldn't have to worry about remembering what all those switches, knobs, dials, and gauges did.

He wouldn't have to remember how to help his brother through all those procedures that they'd made up themselves, or wonder which detail they'd forgotten or which part of the spacecraft might fall off during launch. He wouldn't have to worry about whether the parachutes would open at the right time (or at all), or about his brother getting hit by some space rock while hurtling around the planet. He wouldn't have to worry whether Barry and Howard had accurately calculated the trajectories and guidance parameters, not to mention whether Howard actually knew how to program a computer.

For all any of them knew, Howard might be entering nonsense into the machine and today his brother would end up at the bottom of Greenwood Lake, or on the bottom of the Atlantic Ocean, or pancaked into another continent somewhere on the planet.

Most of all, he wouldn't have to think about how upset their mom and dad would be if something bad happened to Scott.

Mark vowed then and there that he would be a happy-go-lucky TV-watching kid forever after. Cs were fine with him. If his team lost the baseball championship, he wouldn't mind. No more stress and strain. He was not cut out for this.

All this ran through Mark's head—and then one more thing. He wished he were the one going into space. It wasn't that he wanted the glory. All thoughts of glory were long since done with. It wasn't that he wanted the excitement, either. It was just that going into space was the dangerous and lonely part, and he didn't want Scott to have to endure it.

Then he had a final thought: If he didn't know what he had to do by now, he never would. And so it would have to be okay.

Scott, meanwhile, slept like a rock and dreamed about starlight on the ocean; about Planet Earth, the blue color he'd seen in photos from the Apollo moon missions; about the smiling faces of John Glenn and other famous explorers. The images floated by framed in a small square, the outline of the window of *Crazy 8*.

"Christopher Columbus," he murmured, and rolled over.

Barry heard him. He was awake, too, though not quite as anxious as Mark. It wasn't *his* brother who was going to be the first kid in space.

"What? What did you say, Scott?" Barry whispered.

But Scott just murmured something unintelligible and pulled up the covers.

* * *

Egg's research had turned up something interesting about an astronaut's diet: before a mission, they always ate the same breakfast. As the boys got dressed in Twin Territory, the smells coming from the kitchen told them Grandpa Joe was following Egg's menu: steak, eggs, and toast.

A few minutes later, the three boys dropped downstairs and found breakfast on the table. Grandpa himself was standing at the kitchen counter, attempting to pour orange juice through a strainer into a pitcher.

"I'm doing this because Egg told me I had to," he said. "But I'll be darned if I know why."

"It's only Scott that has to have his OJ strained," Mark said. "For Barry and me, it doesn't matter."

"It's for his, uh . . . digestion," Barry said.

"What does orange juice pulp have to do with—?" Grandpa Joe started to ask; then he thought better of it. "Never mind. I don't want to know. Anyway, don't you guys think you're carrying this realism thing a little far?"

The boys looked at one another. Many times in the past couple of weeks, they had come close to telling Grandpa the truth. If any grown-up would understand, he would. The whole thing had been his idea, after all.

But now not one of them felt like they could make that decision. And they hadn't talked it over in advance. So Scott said, "I don't really like the pulp in orange juice that much anyway."

And Barry said, "It's all for Egg and the science fair. She's going to win for sure."

"I don't know about that." Straining done, Grandpa came to the table and poured them each a glass. "Rumor has it Steve Peluso's project is all about fruit flies."

"Ha! Sounds boring," Mark said. "Aren't you gonna eat, Scott?"

"Everything's delicious, Mr. McAvoy," Barry said with his mouth full.

"I'm okay." Scott's plate was still loaded with food.

"I never would've believed you kids could accomplish what you have," Grandpa Joe said. "So I thought I could manage to do my part by getting up early and making breakfast. Now I wish you'd let me go on over to the launch site and watch your whatchamacallit—*dramatization*."

The kids had told Grandpa and the other grown-ups that today's "launch" was really just the "dramatization" of a launch. That was Egg's word. The kids were going to take pictures of Scott climbing the scaffolding and entering the *Crazy 8* capsule as if he were really going to fly. Mission Control was set up in a bunker on the ground, well away from the rocket. Each kid had his or her own responsibilities, and everything each one did would be logged into a notebook. They were taking photos, and Howard's mom had lent them a portable cassette tape recorder, so they could even record comments and radio transmissions.

Only the kids knew that the Drizzle rocket was full of fuel and ready to go.

"Aw, you don't want to do that, Grandpa," Mark said. "It'll be better if you just come to the science fair and look at the pictures on Egg's entry."

NASA began countdowns for Mercury missions at T minus 36—thirty-six hours before launch. Project Blastoff didn't have that luxury. Because the earliest Mrs. O'Malley would agree to drive Egg, Howard, and Lisa over to Grandpa Joe's house was 8:00 a.m., and because launch time was at 9:30, their own countdown was going to start at T-1, or one hour before launch. They would have to hurry, but it seemed like they would have enough time. Just as *Crazy 8* relied on a somewhat simplified design, the launch procedure had been simplified as well.

"Hi, kids! Hi, Peggy. Nice to see you all this morning. Can I interest anybody in some—?" Grandpa said when the O'Malleys' car pulled up and Howard, Lisa, and Egg piled out.

"Good morning, Mr. McAvoy. Thanks, but we gotta hurry," Egg said, staying put in the driveway, which was closer to the launch site than the house was.

"That's all I've heard all morning," said Mrs. O'Malley. "'Hurry, hurry, hurry!' I know the photographs are important, but surely having the angle of sunlight off by this or that small amount isn't really that important. . . ."

"Bye, Mom. Love you. See you after lunch!" Egg was already heading down the driveway and toward the path to the launch site, with Howard and Lisa close behind.

Mark and Barry took off jogging after them. Scott paused in front of his grandfather. "I love you, Grandpa," he said.

Grandpa Joe raised one eyebrow. "Uh . . . well, of course I love you too, Scott."

Mark was at the end of the driveway by this time. He turned back toward the house and walked a few steps backward. "Come *on*, Scott! Bye, Grandpa, see you after lunch."

Without another word, Scott ran after his brother.

Because of the trees and terrain, the kids didn't get a clear view of *Crazy 8* till they came up over the last rise and saw it, looming some fifty feet above them. It was their own creation. They knew every rivet, weld, hose, and switch better than they knew their own fingernails—and even so, they gasped when they saw it in the sunlight.

At the site, each kid had a job and went to his or her station. Scott knew that Howard would be climbing the scaffolding that stood in for the service gantry, providing support and access for the launch vehicle and capsule.

By this time, Howard had made the climb so often, he would ascend like a monkey. On reaching his destination, he would twist two handles to release the outer and inner hatches, pull each open, and swing himself inside, feetfirst. In the tight space, it was his job to do a quick run-through of the *Crazy 8* systems—to wake up the onboard computer; ascertain whether the gauges, sensors, and indicator lights represented reality; ensure that the gyros were properly aligned, that the batteries and environmental system were working, that the fuel levels were full, and that the twelve automatic and six manual thrusters all worked.

When Howard flipped the switch on the cockpit radio, he would say: "Test, test, test?"

From the speaker, Egg's voice would reply. "*Crazy 8*, this is Greenwood Control. We are T minus 30 minutes and counting."

CHAPTER 32

Scott was on his way to change into his flight suit when Egg said, "Wait. What about the prelaunch physical? I need to monitor his health for the science fair entry."

"I'm on it." Lisa pulled a popsicle stick out of her jeans pocket. "Okay, Scott," she said, "turn toward the sun, then open your mouth."

Scott did as he was told. Lisa put the popsicle stick in his mouth, held down his tongue with it, and peered in. Then she shrugged. "I guess that's how a boy's throat is supposed to look. And your breath's okay. How do you feel?"

"Fine."

"Give me your wrist," Lisa said.

"What?"

"Your wrist, so I can take your pulse," Lisa said.

Feeling a little weird about it, Scott handed over his wrist. He was glad the other guys were busy with their checklists. Lisa pressed gently with two fingers, keeping an eye on the second hand of her watch. After thirty seconds, she said, "I count 40, which means 80 beats per minute. For a kid your age, that's a little fast."

"How do you know?" he asked.

"I looked it up," she said. "I am taking my flight surgeon job seriously. Are you freaking out?"

Scott thought about this. "No. I'm kind of excited, is all."

Lisa nodded. "Perfectly normal," she said; then she touched her palm to his forehead.

He protested: *"Hey!"*

"You don't have a fever." She took her hand away and turned to Egg. "I pronounce our astronaut go for launch."

The next order of business was for Scott to put on his suit. He had three minutes to do so, and all went smoothly till the zipper got stuck.

Egg saw his predicament. "Stop tugging it. I'll help."

"Uh . . . that's okay." Scott was embarrassed.

"I got it." Mark stood up and came over. Showing unusual patience, he bent forward, examined the zipper, and with his good right hand, separated the tiny teeth one by one till Scott could pull it the rest of the way.

"Okay, good." Scott stepped back. "I gotta go."

"Yeah, you do," said Mark. For a second, the twins looked at each other. To most people, their faces formed a mirror image. The twins alone saw all the differences.

"Hey, see ya," Scott said at last.

"Yeah," said Mark. "Be careful."

"Uh . . . yeah, I'm kind of counting on you to help with that."

"Right. Okay."

The twins half grinned. They knew they sounded stupid. And they knew there was nothing else to say.

Scott raised his hand to wave, then turned and jogged toward the rocket.

NASA astronauts get an elevator ride to their spacecraft. The Saturn rockets that helped put men on the moon were more than 350 feet—thirty-five stories—tall. The Atlas rocket that launched *Friendship* 7 and the other Mercury flights was about 100 feet tall.

But thanks to Mr. Drizzle's superior design and high-performance "rocket candy" fuel, the *Crazy 8* launch vehicle was comparatively puny, and no elevator was necessary. Grandpa had borrowed an orange painters' scaffolding from a builder friend. It now stood alongside the rocket to enable entry and exit. Scott put his helmet on to free his hands; then, thinking of all the times he had climbed the tree in his front yard, he ascended hand over hand.

On the top of the platform, Barry and Howard were waiting.

"We've gone over every gauge. Every switch is in the right place. Every circuit breaker is closed," Barry said. "The capsule is go!"

"Are you ready?" Howard asked Scott.

Scott gave him a thumbs-up, and Howard smiled one of his rare smiles. "Then get in there!"

The square opening was tiny—each side less than 24 inches in length. Scott took off his helmet and pushed it in ahead of him, then swung his body inside, feetfirst, which was the only way to do it. Astronaut John Glenn had famously said you didn't climb into the Mercury capsule, you tried it on. This was true even if, like Scott, you were a seventy-five-pound kid.

It took some serious maneuvering for Scott to get the helmet back, pull it over his head, and position himself on the seat. As in the simulator, he was now on his back with his knees aimed up. The instrument panel was only a couple of feet from his face, and above it was the small window, now facing west and showing trees and blue sky. All told, the spacecraft packed 120 controls—55 electrical switches, 30 fuses, 35 mechanical levers—and countless circuit breakers.

The hatch was still open, and now Scott heard a sound that must have been Barry's voice—only with his helmet on, Scott couldn't understand the words. He turned his head to say, "What?" but only in time to see the hatch close.

There was a definite thump, and he was alone.

He remembered Lisa's question: "Are you freaking out?"

A little, he thought.

Better get busy.

The first thing on the checklist was to flip the switch that turned on the radio inside his helmet.

"Greenwood Control, this is *Crazy 8*, how do you read?"

"Loud and clear, *Crazy 8*." Mark's voice in his ear was a comfort.

By now it was T-minus-15 minutes. During the time that remained, Scott strapped himself in, centered the attitude control handle, put the guard on the switch to fire the retro rockets, moved the battery switches to on, and retracted the periscope, which looked out from its own little door on the opposite side of the capsule. The controls for the periscope were between his knees.

It wasn't entirely silent in the capsule as he worked. He heard the hiss of the air through the pipes, the hum of the fan, and at one point some bumps that must have meant Egg was swiveling the nozzles on the rocket engine to test them.

Then there was the chatter over the radio—Egg, Lisa,

Barry, and Howard reporting in on the systems for which they were responsible, "Communications, go," "Retro, go," "Guidance, go," "Enviro, go!"

Scott himself was the last item on the list. "*Crazy 8*, this is Greenwood Control. Are you go for launch?"

"I guess," Scott said. "That is—go!"

The minutes counted down and then the seconds— just as they did in training.

The automatic engine starter was due to kick in at T-minus-18 seconds. Scott had wondered how that would feel and soon found out—there was a sound like a crackle and then the faintest jiggle, and then Mark's voice intoning the final countdown: "Seven—six—five— four—three—two—one—ignition!"

Scott just had time to wonder if Mr. Drizzle's rocket candy was for real, if he was actually about to be the first kid in orbit, when—*pow-pow-pow*—the clamps at the base of the rocket released and, with a solid, exciting surge, *Crazy 8* leaped skyward, powered by 360,000 pounds of thrust.

CHAPTER 33

··

When solid fuel ignites, there is instantaneous tooth-rattling vibration. For a second, it seemed to Scott that his spacecraft was coming apart . . . but it held together, and so did he. He glanced at the air speed indicator, located on the old speedometer they had recalibrated, and watched in awe as it ticked upward.

Mark's voice crackled in Scott's ear. "We have liftoff at 2:32.29 p.m. GMT."

The time was 9:32 in the morning in New Jersey. Scott knew GMT stood for Greenwich Mean Time, which is what NASA uses because it's the same everywhere in the world. "Roger," he said. "The clock is running. We are under way."

It seemed to Scott that he had been airborne only a few seconds when the capsule bounced, shuddered, and bounced again. He checked the altimeter: 35,000 feet, Max Q, the point at which the forces buffeting the capsule were greatest and, true to its name, *Crazy 8* reacted by wobbling, bucking, and shimmying.

We built the machine to survive this, Scott reminded himself. It's normal. But at the same time, it had been a lot easier to feel confident when he was in Nando's shop with his feet on the ground and his friends around him.

Barry had calculated the flight path that would put the capsule into its orbit; Howard had programmed the electronic guidance system to follow it. For now, Scott was just along for the ride as *Crazy 8* shot straight up. Twenty seconds after liftoff, Scott reported that altimeter, clock, and compass readings were good. Mark didn't answer right away, and Scott tried again: "Greenwood Control? *Crazy 8.* Come in please."

Static crackled in his ear, and then . . . strange sounds: a wailing siren, a confused tangle of shouts.

Am I imagining things? Scott wondered. "Greenwood Control, do you—?"

"Yeah, I'm here," said Mark. He sounded breathless, but continued, "I'm fine. That is, Roger. We have a visual on your flight path, and it looks good."

Scott wanted to ask about the noises on the ground but decided he had better things to do. Stay focused. Stay busy. Using tables prepared by Lisa, he cross-checked altitude, air speed, and pitch attitude to ensure he was continuously on course. He was. Just the way it was supposed to, the capsule rose vertically for thirty seconds before arcing gradually to the east.

Everything looked fine and then—only half a minute later—the ride smoothed out and the Gs began to build, pushing Scott against his seat with the force of an invisible six-hundred-pound gorilla until, as if he'd crested the top of the roller coaster, the force began to drop, drop, and drop until, at five minutes after launch, Scott was weightless—and entering orbit 100 miles above Earth.

Scott took a deep breath, the first in a while, then heard three little popgun pops, each of which bumped the spacecraft forward.

"Greenwood Control, *Crazy 8*. Engine cutoff and the posigrades have fired."

"Roger, *Crazy 8*. That's great news."

Having done its job, the Drizzle rocket had shut down and separated from the capsule. Now the capsule performed a turn so that the blunt end—the one protected by the heat shield—was in front.

Scott was overcome by a host of sensations.

Where a moment ago an invisible gorilla had sat on his chest, now he was floating in his harness. It was a little like being buoyed by water—only there was no water—and surprisingly, after a few moments, it didn't even seem that strange. As an experiment, he let go of the pencil in his hand and watched, fascinated, as it floated and spun in the air.

Then there was the view. Once the capsule had turned around, the periscope with its eight-inch eyepiece had extended. Now Scott could look down through the eyepiece and see for hundreds of miles in every direction: the sun's clear light on white clouds; patches of brilliant blue water—the Atlantic Ocean. Behind him, the brown-and-green coastline of the United States receded, as did the Drizzle rocket, beginning its own descent into the water. He could look out the window, too, and it was just incredible.

"Greenwood Control, *Crazy 8*. Wow!"

"Wow what? Is everything okay?" Mark sounded worried.

"Roger, everything's fine. It's just really beautiful up here. Earth is like a big blue ball, and it floats—it's just floating there in space."

He knew he probably sounded pretty stupid, but he didn't care.

"*Crazy 8*, Greenwood Control. Oh—good to hear. Hey, you know you'll be dipping below the horizon soon. That'll put you out of radio range. While we can still talk, Egg wants you to know she left you a surprise in the ditty bag."

A surprise? What could possibly be surprising now?

"Roger, Greenwood Control. I'll check."

The ditty bag, stowed in a compartment by his left thigh, contained emergency essentials like a flashlight and a knife. Now he opened the compartment, and the bag rose like an obedient ghost to meet him. Inside, besides the items he expected, he found a plastic sandwich bag full of cookies. Check that. It *used* to be full of cookies. Unfortunately, Max Q, not to mention all those Gs, had been hard on them, and what he held was a bag of crumbs.

"*Crazy 8*, Greenwood Control. Did you find the present?"

"That's affirmative, Greenwood Control. Uh . . . uh-oh." Before he could stop them, a swarm of chocolate chip gravel escaped the bag and began to find its way everywhere. Shoot! How was he going to get the crumbs back in the bag? Every time he caught some, more escaped. He seemed to be engaged in a cookie gravel battle of epic proportions.

Frustrated, Scott said, "Nice thought, Greenwood, but the cookies got crushed and it's kind of a mess, actually."

"*Crazy 8*, Greenwood. So sorry. Next time we'll send a vacuum cleaner."

It's not funny, Scott thought, batting at the cloud, which was a mistake because it just caused the crumbs to spread out more widely. Those guys on the ground don't get that it's different in space, and all this mess could cause a problem.

Suddenly, he felt very far away.

"Greenwood Control, *Crazy 8*. Do you read? The view is really beautiful from up here. I can see the East Coast of the United States south to Georgia, I think."

No answer.

"Greenwood Control?"

No answer.

So that was it. T-plus-10 minutes and he was out of radio range. NASA astronauts had a network of communication centers all over the world, so they were almost never without company and support, not to mention that there was radar monitoring of every move. Project Blastoff did not have such luxuries. Scott was traveling east and for the next hour or so—till he reached the West Coast of the United States—he was really on his own.

CHAPTER 34

Scott knew he was traveling at around 17,500 miles per hour, that daylight would last about forty minutes, and that night would last the same. Watching the Atlantic rush by below him, he thought about being an object in motion, a satellite in orbit around Earth.

According to Newton's first law, an object in motion stays in motion unless something else interferes. In this case two things interfered. One was atmosphere. It was thin at that altitude but still present. The other was gravity, pulling the spacecraft back toward Earth. Orbit is the balancing act between the satellite's straight-line momentum and gravity's pull.

Scott thought of Astronaut Bill Anders's response to a kindergartner who asked which astronaut was driving *Apollo 8*, the first NASA mission to orbit the moon.

Anders had said that none of the astronauts was driving. Mr. Isaac Newton was.

Having studied an atlas, Scott recognized the west coast of Africa when it appeared below him, with sand dunes and dust storms on the desert and everywhere clouds of all sizes, shapes, and colors. A few moments later he saw a sight very familiar from geography— Italy's boot-shaped peninsula jutting into the blue Mediterranean Sea.

Most beautiful of all was sunset over the Indian Ocean, right on schedule at T-plus-43 minutes. Glowing with blue-white intensity, the nearest star dropped Earthward, creating a brilliant display of orange, red, purple, and blue stripes fading into black space. Above, the sky shone with white dots, the steadily burning stars.

Scott had known to expect the stars' steady gaze. It's only interference from Earth's atmosphere that makes them twinkle, and he was above that interference now. The transformation of something familiar—starlight— into something strange made Scott feel even more alone.

How would he ever be able to describe it?

Meanwhile, the radio was quiet but the capsule was not. There was the faint, steady *shhh* of air flowing in the environmental control system, the clicking of the gyros as they moved in the IMU, and the occasional *ssss* of the hydrogen peroxide–powered nozzles on the thrusters outside, firing intermittently to keep the capsule steady.

Reaction engines, Scott thought, and said another silent thanks to Mr. Newton.

It could be there's only so much grandeur a kid can take in. Over the Pacific, Scott decided to do a little flying on his own. This required toggling the manual panel switch to on and taking the control stick in his right hand. Aligning the horizon display on the periscope with Earth's horizon, he tugged and twisted the stick to move the capsule up, down, right, left, and sideways, listening to the sound of the little thrusters firing outside.

He had done a decent job of imitating them during the sims with Mark in their bedroom, he decided.

Scott knew he wouldn't knock himself out of orbit. Instead, he was changing *Crazy 8*'s attitude—spinning, twisting, and pivoting it within the bounds of its trajectory. The Mercury astronauts had had their troubles keeping their capsules' attitudes on target, but so far *Crazy 8* had done fine.

The shortest night of Scott's life was soon over. If the stars of deep space had been eerie, sunlit Earth seemed alive and inviting. Space travel, Scott thought, was thrilling—but looking Earthward, he felt the emotional pull of home like the physical pull of gravity.

For comfort, he opened the faceplate on his helmet, reached out, and awkwardly, with his gloved right hand, grabbed a handful of the cookie dust and brought it to his mouth. Delicious—but he wished he had milk to go with it.

Scott checked the clock. It was T-plus-65 minutes—already time to implement the re-entry checklist, which began: Check your seat belt.

Re-entry was the most dangerous part of the trip. As *Crazy 8* descended, it would leave the near vacuum of space and hit the thickening atmosphere at high speed. The friction between air and spacecraft would create a heat pulse around the capsule with a temperature close to 5,000 degrees Fahrenheit, almost as hot as the sun.

Only the heat shield and the aeronautic design of the capsule protected him.

And if something was to go wrong?

He would be a crispy critter, and *Crazy 8* a meteor that flashed for an instant, then disappeared.

Approaching California, the automatic system went to work, moving *Crazy 8* to proper attitude and activating re-entry control. The three retrorockets fired one after the other, each slowing velocity by 500 feet per second. In his seat, Scott felt them like shoves from a ghostly hand.

These three burns were supposed to set him on a path for Greenwood Lake. If they succeeded, Barry and Howard—who had done the math and the programming—truly were geniuses.

Meanwhile, with every action of the electronic control, the appropriate indicator light flashed yellow, then green, to say all was well.

And then—suddenly—all was not well. Instead of turning green, one of the yellow lights, the one for periscope operation, turned red.

Had the periscope failed to retract? Was it stuck? Was the door still open?

The light did not offer details. Scott peered down into the eyepiece and saw only gray. The door seemed to be closed. But if it was open even the merest crack, the superheated plasma created on re-entry would leak inside—destroying *Crazy 8* and Scott Kelly, too.

CHAPTER 35

They had trained for this. They had trained for everything.

As a result, Scott knew exactly what to do. Calmly, he reached between his knees and grasped the periscope's manual control handle. Pumping it would override the electronic system.

Except . . . the handle was stuck, wouldn't budge a millimeter.

And the red light stayed lit.

"Greenwood Control, *Crazy 8*. Come in, Greenwood Control. I've got a problem. Over."

There was a crackle in the speaker and then—what a wonderful sound—his brother's voice: "Go ahead, *Crazy 8*—and it's great to hear you!"

"Roger," Scott said, "great to hear you, too, but listen." Then he described the situation.

"*Crazy 8.*" Mark's voice was steady. "Stand by for instructions."

How long? Scott thought. And the next few seconds were the longest of his life. Then came Mark's voice again. "*Crazy 8*, Greenwood Control. Did you say something about cookie crumbs?"

By this time, cookie crumbs were the furthest thing from Scott's mind, but he answered, "Uh, that's affirmative."

In the background, Scott could hear an unfamiliar voice. Who was it? Then Mark's voice again. "*Crazy 8*, can you try something? Can you get down there and see if maybe there are crumbs in the mechanism?"

Scott's first thought was, No way. Unhook his harness? Climb around the spaceship? Flip upside down? *Now?*

Scott's second thought was he didn't have a better idea. "Roger. I understand."

Wasting no time, Scott unbuckled his harness, rolled himself into a ball, flipped over, and extended his hands. In the tight space he was brutally uncomfortable, and it didn't help that the capsule was starting to bounce.

Scott knew the exact location of the periscope door; he had installed it himself. Still, it was hard to find in the darkness created by his own shadow, and he felt for it blindly. Then he remembered the mini flashlights on the index fingers of each glove, put there so he could locate switches at night. He twisted them to on and seconds later located the hinge.

Cookie crumbs!

A smear of them had settled in exactly the wrong place, literally gumming up the works. He reached, but the capsule chose that moment to jump; his helmet hit the underside of the control panel, twisting his neck— *ouch!* There was no time to worry about little things like his head or his neck, though. With every second, *Crazy 8* fell faster. He had to get himself buckled in—but he had to get the periscope door closed first.

Using his right glove for light, he stretched mightily toward the floor, barely managing to swipe the crumbs with his fingertips.

The crumbs floated toward him but slowly, already influenced by Earth's gravitational pull.

Had it worked? Had he cleared the hinge? All he could do was swipe once more, then flip back over, uncurl his torso, push against the seat, and buckle himself in. He was sweating and exhausted when for the second time he grabbed the periscope handle and pushed with all his might.

Oh, gosh—still stuck. Death by cookie crumbs? It would be just too stupid. With another mighty effort, he pushed again and made the handle move, pushed again and again till finally, at last, it seemed the mechanism was free.

Scott turned his head—*ow*, his neck hurt—to look at the panel to his left.

Yes!

The light was green!

He buckled himself back in, every muscle in his body limp with relief. Then he spoke: "Greenwood Control? *Crazy 8*. Do you read?"

"Roger, *Crazy 8*. Go a—" And then static. For the four minutes of re-entry coinciding with maximum heat, the cloud of ionized particles outside the capsule cut off all radio contact. Effectively, Scott was now at the center of a fireball—and no one could hear him.

Through the window, Scott could see a bright orange glow punctuated by flashes as the plasma interacted with the spacecraft. He was scared. If he was wrong about the periscope door—or if any of a thousand other things had gone wrong—he would die. For him it would be over very fast.

But what about his family? Would his parents blame Mark? Would they blame Grandpa?

All in all, it would be a whole lot better to survive.

"Greenwood Control? Greenwood Control? This is *Crazy 8*. How do you receive? Over."

No answer. No answer, and the seconds ticked by.

Then, at last: "Roger, *Crazy 8*. Loud and clear! How are you doing?"

"Oh, pretty good," Scott said, "considering."

True, the invisible gorilla was back—but hey, no problem.

Crazy 8's descent continued. At 20,000 feet, the capsule began to sway, and the small parachute called a drogue deployed automatically to steady it. Then, at 10,000 feet, Scott saw the main chute open up and felt a jolt as it ballooned above him. For five glorious minutes, he floated toward the surface of Greenwood Lake—back where he'd begun only ninety minutes before.

It was 4:03.03 GMT when water splashed the capsule window and Scott sent his last transmission as an astronaut: "Greenwood Control, *Crazy 8*. I've landed, and fortunately this thing floats."

CHAPTER 36

In his brain, Scott knew he had only been out of this world for an hour and a half—not even as long as the running time of his favorite movie, *Jaws*. But still he couldn't bring himself to believe it. Everything had changed—from the way Grandpa's boat felt bobbing on the water to his view of the sky above, blue because of the refraction of sunlight on the atmosphere, not black the way it had been only a few minutes ago.

Scott would have thought this wasn't the homecoming he had imagined, except he realized that he hadn't imagined any homecoming at all. There had been no room in his mind for it. In fact, the normal milestones a kid looked forward to in the fall—things like the Giants and the Jets, Thanksgiving, Christmas vacation—he hadn't thought of at all. For months all that had mattered was overcoming the technical problems of putting a kid into orbit.

Now, suddenly it became clear that there was life after orbiting the Earth, and that surprised him more than the sight onshore before him: a zillion flashing lights on what seemed like an equal number of police vehicles. A helicopter was circling overhead. And his grandfather, steering the powerboat toward shore, was saying something. He seemed to be excited. What was he talking about?

He was glad to see Scott in one piece—Scott got that much. There were tears in his eyes, Scott noticed. Scott had never seen his grandfather cry before.

"What's going on?" Scott said at last, interrupting his grandfather in midsentence. By this time, he had pulled off his helmet. Turning his head, he could see the *Crazy 8* capsule bobbing in the middle of the lake.

"That's what I've been trying to explain!" Grandpa Joe was too happy to be exasperated. "There's been a little problem. Steve Peluso snooped in Egg's project notebook, and—"

"That sneak!" Scott said.

"Well, some might argue that *that's* a case of the pot calling the kettle black," Grandpa said.

"Point taken," said Scott. "So then what happened?"

"He and his dad and the cops arrived right about the same time the capsule was disappearing into the wild blue yonder."

So that was the siren I heard, Scott thought, and the voices in the background of Mark's radio transmissions. He didn't tell me because he didn't want to distract me, and anyway, there was nothing I could do.

"And there's something else about Steve Peluso that might soften your anger some," Grandpa said.

Scott doubted it. "What's that?"

"He was the one who suggested there might be crumbs in the hinge of the periscope door," Grandpa said. "He remembered he read something about crumbs on *Aurora* 7—one of the Mercury flights."

By now they were nearing the shore. "Look," Grandpa said, "before all heck breaks loose, I just want to say something. I never thought you'd pull it off. And no one else did either. Right about now, I'd like to whip all of you, or at least send you to sit on a hard stool in a tight corner. But I have to say, I am darned proud."

"Thank you," Scott said. "But"—he gestured toward the lakeshore—"I guess we're in trouble, right?"

Grandpa nodded toward the lights, the vehicles, and the uniformed men and women who were waiting. "Uh, yeah. I'd say so."

"Mom and Dad?" Scott didn't really want to know the answer.

"They're on their way," Grandpa said.

CHAPTER 37

Mark and Scott never knew there were so many government agencies in the universe that you could get in trouble with—the town police, the county sheriff, the state police, the FBI, the NTSB, the FAA, the FCC, the U.S. Department of State, EPA, NASA, and even the New Jersey state park system.

For a while, they thought at least they weren't in trouble with the truant officer because they had flown their mission on a weekend. But then they found out Egg's school district had a rule that you couldn't violate the law in the course of preparing your science fair entry. That really was written down. Steve Peluso's father had found the paragraph.

Mr. and Mrs. Kelly's reaction to the twins' adventure had been much like Grandpa Joe's—equal parts pride and fury, which resolved to disbelief. In the days after the Crazy 8 mission, Mark and Scott noticed that very often their parents looked at them, opened their mouths to say something, blinked, closed their mouths, shook their heads, and shrugged.

The overall result was a quieter than usual Kelly household—as if the family was waiting breathlessly for something, but what?

The twins and Barry had been greeted as celebrities when they first went back to school. Kids who weren't really Scott's or Mark's friends had taken to calling each of them "Astrotwin" in the hall, partly because they couldn't remember which one had gone up in space and partly because kids who didn't know them well had a hard time telling them apart. This lasted a week, and then Sharon Gladstone came back from a trip to the Jersey Shore with an autograph from this new young singer—Bruce Springsteen his name was—and that was all anybody wanted to talk about.

Because of the science fair, things were different for Egg, Howard, and Lisa. With his flair for showmanship, Mr. Drizzle recognized that after the TV coverage of the flight, their participation in it would draw a big crowd.

"Whatever risks those kids took," he told the principal, "their mission was definitely educational. Besides, if we put them on the flyer, we'll break every attendance record."

The principal agreed, and so did the school board.

Jenny O'Malley's entry could be displayed with the others in the gym, provided it was disqualified from competition.

This explained why the team found itself reunited in the West Milford Elementary School gym two weeks after the successful flight of *Crazy 8*. Outside at the curb were parked television news trucks from the major networks, and local stations, too.

Under the circumstances, the kids didn't know exactly how to behave. They wanted to slap backs and grin and talk about all they'd overcome, the thrill of seeing the spacecraft lift off, the relief at seeing Scott back safe.

They wanted to ask Scott all the questions they hadn't had a chance to ask him on launch day.

On the other hand, they knew they were still in trouble, and they could maybe get themselves into more trouble if someone like the principal thought they were being too rowdy.

Mr. Drizzle positioned them behind the table that supported Egg's display, which was a trifold with blueprints of *Crazy 8*, a picture of John Glenn and *Friendship 7*, photographs of the building process in Grandpa's workshop and of Mission Control. Mr. Perez had stuck a copy of Nando's business card in a corner so people knew where they should take their cars if they needed repairing.

Unfortunately, the display did not include the *Crazy 8* module, because it had been confiscated by the authorities the moment it was fished out of the lake.

And it didn't include the Drizzle rocket, which was somewhere at the bottom of the Atlantic Ocean. As for Mr. Drizzle's rocket fuel recipe, he was in negotiations to transfer it to NASA.

Steve Peluso's fruit fly experiment, with a big blue ribbon attached, was across from Egg's, and he was also there to answer questions—not that anyone was interested. When he smiled a sheepish smile at the twins, they nodded back. They didn't like him. He was a sneak. At the same time, they knew what they owed him.

"He saved your rear end," Mark said to Scott.

"I know," Scott said gloomily. "Have you talked to him?" he asked Egg.

Egg scowled. "Yeah. My mom made me. I think he wants to be friends."

"Yuck," said Mark.

"I know," said Egg.

All morning long, the kids stood in a row, answering questions, while Mr. Drizzle—a big grin on his face—kept the line of smiling spectators moving: "One question per person, please, and absolutely no autographs."

Of course, the reporters insisted that they should have a chance to ask more than a single question, and

Scott soon got used to answering them:

"Thank you, yes, it was really exciting. Uh . . . like riding a bucking bronco, that's how it felt when it launched. No, actually I never have ridden a bucking bronco.

"Uh, Earth looked mostly blue, very bright blue. And the Pacific Ocean is really, really big.

"Uh . . . yes, I guess I *did* gain a new appreciation for how our world is just floating in space, so we better take care of it.

"Uh-huh, you're right. Building a spacecraft is hard. No, I wouldn't really recommend it as a summer project. It doesn't leave time for much else."

When Scott was done with a reporter, he always said, "You should really talk to my brother, Mark, and to Jenny and Barry and Howard and Lisa. What they did is at least as important as what I did."

Some of the reporters followed through, but a lot wanted only to file their stories and move on after hearing from the boy astronaut himself.

Mark decided he didn't mind not being the celebrity. He had always been the more talkative of the two brothers—the know-it-all, as Scott liked to say. It was kind of entertaining to see Scott take on that job for once.

The fair was over at noon, and Mrs. O'Malley invited all the kids, Grandpa Joe, and Mr. Drizzle to Egg's house for lunch. The house turned out to be really nice, like the kind of house a rich person would have. A huge yard. A circular driveway. Matching furniture that looked new. Fluffy wall-to-wall carpeting. Real paintings, and mirrors with gold frames on the wall.

Mr. and Mrs. Kelly had taught the boys not to be impressed by money. What really mattered about a person was honesty, kindness, and a good work ethic.

Still, it was hard not to feel impressed . . . and a little envious of Egg, who got to live there.

The boys realized they didn't know much about Mrs. O'Malley. Did she have a job?

And what about Mr. O'Malley? Was he dead? Away on business? Working on an old car out back?

Lunch was set on the big table in the formal dining room. They were getting ready to sit down when Barry excused himself to go to the bathroom.

"It's down the hall to the left." Grandpa Joe pointed.

Scott and Mark looked at each other. Scott said, "Grandpa, have you been here before?"

"Once or twice," said Grandpa Joe vaguely.

Everyone sat down, but an empty chair remained. Then the doorbell rang, and Mrs. O'Malley answered it. When she came back to the dining room, she brought Steve Peluso with her.

"Hi, everybody." He looked nervous. "Sorry I'm late. I rode my bike."

He took the empty chair.

"Mom?" Egg said.

"Have some lunch," Mrs. O'Malley said. "I'll explain after we eat."

This, the twins agreed, was an excellent idea. There was pepperoni pizza, apple pie, and ice cream. There were carrot and celery sticks, too, served with a dipping bowl of something called ranch dressing. It reminded everyone of extra-salty mayonnaise.

While they ate, Mr. Drizzle, Mrs. O'Malley, and Grandpa kept up a steady stream of boring conversation, the kind grown-ups specialize in.

As lunch began to wind down, Mrs. O'Malley said, "You kids are awfully quiet."

No one replied right away, and Grandpa chuckled. "I think, Peggy, they're still worrying about when the ax is going to fall."

"Is that it?" she asked. "Because if so, I can reassure you. You kids did something at least as foolish as it was brave, but we are all very proud of you."

"Here, here!" Mr. Drizzle raised his glass of milk in a toast.

At the same time, Steve Peluso spoke up. "Wait a sec. I don't want to take credit for something I didn't do."

"It's true you didn't help us build the spacecraft," Egg said. "And it's true you called the police on us. But still, we owe you big-time. Without you, Scott might not be here today."

"Precisely," said Mrs. O'Malley. "And one more thing—the one you're going to think is most important. None of you is going to get in trouble."

Mark hadn't realized how anxious he was till his anxiety lifted, and it felt like a headache going away. But Scott was more puzzled than relieved. When he looked around, he realized everyone else was confused too—but none of the kids wanted to be the first to admit they didn't understand what was going on.

Thank goodness for Howard, who didn't care what anyone thought of him.

"Why aren't we in trouble?" he asked.

Mrs. O'Malley smiled. "Certain people are impressed with what you accomplished, and they believe your skills, knowledge, talent, and tenacity might be useful to the space program in the future. As for your current legal predicament, these people have enough influence to squelch any charges that might be brought against you—provided you are willing to sign on."

"You mean sign on to more space exploration?" Egg said.

The kids looked at one another. For his part, Scott couldn't believe his luck. He had assumed he'd never fly in space again—and now maybe he would.

It was quiet for a moment while everyone else let Mrs. O'Malley's words sink in. What were they thinking?

At last, Egg spoke: "Yes!"

Then Steve Peluso: "Yes! Uh, provided I'm invited."

"Space walks! The moon! Mars!" said Barry. "Is everybody else in, too?"

They all answered in the affirmative . . . except Mark.

Hadn't he sworn he never wanted to do anything this hard or this stressful again? That from now on there'd be no more studying math and physics till all hours, or taking lengthy trips to the library, or learning to arc-weld?

An endless life of cartoons, potato chips, and the Yankees in summer is what he wanted to look forward to. That was the life for him.

Wasn't it?

But all of a sudden he remembered how excited he felt when he saw *Crazy 8* on the launch pad, when he saw it lift off just as they'd planned. He remembered the satisfaction of being part of Greenwood Control and understanding the forces that made the flight possible. He remembered the thrill, the relief, of seeing his brother return safe.

It had been worth it, he now realized—even when he was afraid they'd all go to jail, it had been worth it.

Everyone was looking at him, and he grinned. "I'm in, but there is one thing."

"What's that?" Scott asked.

Mark waved the cast on his arm. "Next time, *I'm* going to be the astronaut."

Author's Note

Project Blastoff is fiction, a made-up story. As eleven-year-olds in New Jersey in 1975, my brother, Scott, and I pulled some crazy stunts, but we never actually built a spacecraft in Grandpa's barn and launched it into orbit.

There are a whole bunch of reasons no kid—not even my brother and I—could have done this, but the unbeatable engineering problem is concocting fuel that is powerful enough. While rocket candy is for real and used for launching model rockets all the time, Mr. Drizzle's supercharged secret formula does not, as of this writing, exist.

Beyond that the scientific and mathematical principles described in the story are factual as is the historical background on NASA missions. Most importantly, the story accurately depicts the hard work, cooperation, and brainpower required for any adventure as ambitious as space travel.

In the Glossary that follows are some definitions I hope will help with your own understanding of what it takes to launch anyone into orbit, as well as some suggestions for further reading.

Mark Kelly
September 2014

Glossary

Apollo-Soyuz (page 18): This was the first international manned space-flight, and it took place in the summer of 1975. The *Apollo* spacecraft, belonging to the United States, docked with a *Soyuz* craft, belonging to what was then the Soviet Union. The two countries historically had many disagreements, so it was important to world peace that they jointly planned and carried out a space mission.

Atoms (page 140): Tiny, basic units of matter, invisible to the naked eye.

Attitude (page 145): How an object is oriented in three dimensions, for example whether it is rolled one way or the other, facing right or left, or tilting up and down.

Buoyancy (page 70): The force of a fluid, like water, on an object in it, like a boat or a swimmer. If something floats, it is because of buoyancy.

Central Processing Unit, CPU (page 2): The computer's brain, which can be compared to the one in your head. A person thinks about information; a CPU processes data.

Combustion (page 139): The production of light and heat when certain substances combine. Burning is a form of combustion. The forces of combustion can be used to make cars, rockets, and other vehicles move.

Compression (page 60): In this case, what happens to the air in a hollow rubber ball (a basketball, for example) when the surface hitting the ground flattens briefly, shrinking the space inside. As the compressed air presses the rubber back to its original shape, it adds to the ball's bounce.

Friction (page 55): When two things rub against each other, that's friction. The things don't have to be objects. They can be a baseball moving through air or a boat moving through water. When there is friction, there is resistance, so friction slows down an object in motion.

G-forces (page 111): These are measurements of acceleration, which means the rate at which something moves faster. A force of 1-g means acceleration is the same as that caused by Earth's gravity. Astronauts in a spacecraft accelerating at greater than 1-g are pressed against their seats and feel heavier than normal.

Galileo (page 67): Galileo Galilei was an Italian mathematician, astronomer, philosopher, and scientist who lived from 1564–1642. He built a telescope and made important discoveries about the sun and planets. Like Newton, he wrote about motion and how different forces affect objects.

Gravitational pull (page 67): The attractive force caused by gravity. All objects have this, but because it's weak, it's most noticeable in the case of huge objects like stars and planets, and especially Earth.

Gravity (page 55): A force that causes all objects to attract one another. The pull of gravity is in proportion to an object's mass. Because Earth has more mass than the Moon, an astronaut weighs more on Earth than he or she does on the Moon.

Gyroscope (page 144): A gyroscope is a device made up of an axle that is free to move any which way, and a wheel that spins around it. Because of the principles of angular momentum, the wheel's spin enables the device to measure how the axle is placed in space (its orientation). A gyroscope is at the heart of the system that keeps a spacecraft stable.

Hydrocarbons (page 140): Hydrocarbons are chemicals made up of two elements, hydrogen and carbon. Elements are the most basic substances. Because of the way they combine with oxygen, hydrocarbons make good fuels.

M=D•V (page 57): This equation says that mass is equal to density multiplied times volume. It describes the relationship between mass (which, in the everyday world, is the same as matter or, very loosely, stuff), density (how tightly packed together the matter is) and volume (how big the space is in which the matter is packed). Mass is not the same as weight because weight changes depending on the force of gravity exerted on an object, and mass does not.

Methane, kerosene, and gasoline (page 140): Three chemicals that combust in a way that makes them useful as fuels.

Moore's Law (page 52): In 1965 computer pioneer Gordon Moore predicted that hardware advances would enable computer processors to become twice as fast *and* twice as small every two years. He was pretty much right.

Newton (page 60): Sir Isaac Newton was an English scientist and mathematician who lived from 1643–1727. Among his books was Mathematical Principles of Natural Philosophy, which many people believe is the most important scientific book ever written. It formed the basis for modern physics and showed how gravity applies to all objects.

Nitrogen tetroxide propellant (page 14): A gas used to power thrusters—small rockets—that make up the reaction control system (RCS). It is poisonous.

Reaction Control System, RCS (page 14): Several thrusters—small rockets—that make adjustments in a spacecraft's placement in space (orientation) so that it moves as it should to get where it's going. In the case of the Apollo-Soyuz mission, the poisonous gas inside one of the thrusters leaked into the crew compartment, briefly endangering *Apollo* astronauts.

Rocket equation (page 87): This equation describes the motion of an object (like a rocket) that is being pushed along by fuel as the fuel burns up and the object's mass shrinks. It was published in 1903 by a Russian teacher and scientist, Konstantin Tsiolkovsky.

Specific impulse (page 141): A measure of the amount of power the propellant in an engine can deliver over a particular period of time. To move a rocket from Earth into space, the fuel needs a high specific impulse. It can also be thought of as the amount of thrust you get from accelerating a pound of mass through the nozzle of a rocket motor.

Trajectory (page 182): The path along which something, like a spacecraft, arrow. or baseball, is moving after it has been set in motion.

Velocity (page 88): Similar to speed, it means how fast or slow an object moves in one direction. So if speed stays the same but direction changes, then velocity changes.

Suggested Reading

(Written for young children)

Aldrin, Buzz and Minor, Wendell, *Reaching for the Moon*, New York: HarperCollins, 2005. A picture-book autobiography of one of the first men to walk on the Moon.

Floca, Brian, *Moonshot*, New York: Atheneum, 2009. The story of Apollo 11, the first manned flight to the moon, told in picture-book form with lots of helpful diagrams.

Kelly, Mark and Payne, C. F., *Mousetronaut*, New York: Simon & Schuster/Paula Wiseman Books, 2012, and *Mousetronaut Goes to Mars*, New York: Simon & Schuster/Paula Wiseman Books, 2013. Fictionalized stories based on the smallest, bravest mouse that flew on the space shuttle *Endeavour*.

McNulty, Faith, and Kellogg, Stephen, *If You Decide to Go to the Moon*, New York: Scholastic, 2005. Everything from flight preparations to splashdown is covered in this mock how-to manual.

Suggested Reading

(Written for older children and adults)

Carpenter, M. Scott, et. al., *We Seven: By the Astronauts Themelves*, New York: Simon & Schuster, 1962. Each of the seven *Mercury* astronauts tell their stories.

Collins, Michael, *Carrying the Fire: An Astronaut's Journey*, New York: Adventure Library 1974. Apollo 11 pilot and later Air and Space Museum director, Collins is a terrific writer.

Kranz, Gene, *Failure is Not an Option*, New York: Simon & Schuster 2000. Gene Kranz, former NASA flight director, recounts his NASA experiences from Mercury to Apollo and beyond.

Zimba, Jason, *Force + Motion*, Baltimore: Johns Hopkins University Press 2009. A guide that explains Newton's laws of motion in visual terms.

On the web:
http://www.nasa.gov/audience/forstudents/ has information on current and past NASA missions.

Turn the page for a sneak peek at

Astrotwins—Project Rescue

SaTURDaY, MaRCH 28, 1976

Mark Kelly was doing his best to save his dog's life, but his dog—a big brown mutt named Major Nelson—did not want to be saved. Again and again, Mark fastened the clear plastic oxygen mask over his nose. Again and again, Major Nelson shook it off.

"Can I get some help here?" Mark asked his twin brother, Scott.

It was after lunch, and the two twelve-year-olds were kneeling on the carpet in the living room of their house. Sprawled between them, Major Nelson thumped his tail; dog rescue was the best game yet!

"If I help, it'll spoil my entertainment," Scott said. "You're better than watching *Happy Days* on TV."

The boys had a real oxygen mask, one with perforations to allow air flow. But in place of an oxygen tank, they were using a big soda bottle, its cap replaced by a valve made out of cardboard discs. For tubing, they had taped together plastic drinking straws. The flimsy homemade setup didn't look very realistic, but it gave the boys a way to practice for tests in their Red Cross first aid class—or, for that matter, real emergencies.

"You are not very funny," Mark told Scott. "Now do me a favor and keep the mask on his nose while I hook everything up."

Scott did as his brother directed while at the same time scratching Major Nelson behind the ears. "You're a good dog—yes, you are!"

"Woof," Major Nelson agreed.

"Ha!" Mark pumped his fist. "He's connected! How long did that take, do you think?"

Scott shook his head and sighed. "Too long. Our dog is dead."

"Oh, cut it out," Mark said. "Maybe when Mom gets home she'll let us practice on her."

"You know she'll say she's too busy," Scott said. "And besides, we don't have that much time. We gotta meet Barry at the library at two thirty."

Mark made a face. "I forgot about that. Can you believe we have to go to the library? *Again?*"

"I know. I thought we were done with libraries forever after all the research we did last summer. But if we're going to write that report, we need to," Scott said.

Mark's face brightened. "I just thought of something. Barry's a brainiac! He can do all the hard parts, and we'll just draw pictures or something."

"You? Draw pictures?" Scott said.

"Yeah, okay, *you* draw the pictures," Mark said. "And I'll, uh . . . write my name on the top. How does that sound?"

"You probably can't screw up writing your name," said Scott, "even if you did suffocate Major Nelson."

"Don't blame me. The mask was made for a human, not a canine," Mark said.

"We could practice on each other," Scott said, "and since it's my turn, you're the one who has to lie down, be quiet, and pretend you're supersick. Ready—go!"

Mark shook his head. "Like I'm gonna let you press that thing on my face! Why would I even trust you?"

"Uh . . . because I'm the only brother you've got? And I trusted you when I went into space last fall."

"At least you had a clean faceplate on your helmet," said Mark. "This mask is gross—covered with dog drool."

"Woof," said Major Nelson.

"Aw, look, you've hurt his feelings." Scott waved the mask as if he was about to clamp it over his brother's nose, his brother swerved out of the way, Scott hooked him by the elbow, Mark lunged, and an instant later the two boys were on the floor, wrestling . . . much to the delight of Major Nelson, who howled his encouragement.

The match, punctuated by thumps, bumps, and grunts, came to an abrupt end when Mom appeared in the doorway. "Boys?"

Mark was out of breath but still managed to say, "He started it!"

Scott, also breathless, objected: "That's not true!"

"Oh yeah?" Mark said. "You can ask Major Nelson, Mom. He saw the whole thing."

"Well, maybe I did start it," Scott admitted, "but I'm not the one with a bad attitude about first-aid class."

"At least I practice," Mark said. "You just sit back and watch."

"Yeah—watch you suffocate patients," Scott said. "I just hope to heck you never have to save anybody for real, 'cause if you do, they're done for."

"Hold on a second." Mom had been eyeing her sons from the doorway. Now she came into the room and sat down on the sofa. "I thought you guys liked the class."

"We do," Scott said quickly.

"Said the kiss-up," said Mark.

"I am not a kiss-up," said Scott.

"Yeah, you are," said Mark.

Mom raised her hand. "Leaving that aside for now—what gives with the class?"

"It's just we're never gonna have to use this stuff," Mark said.

Scott chimed in. "Nobody counts on kids to save lives,

Mom. They count on doctors and nurses and ambulance people. They count on cops sometimes. But we're not old enough for those jobs."

Mom cocked her head and smiled. "This line of reasoning's kind of funny coming from you two."

Mark by this time had sat up and assessed his injuries. There seemed to be a bruise on his shoulder and another on his head, but that was okay. He was pretty sure he had given as good as he got. "What do you mean?" he asked his mom.

"I think she means the whole space thing," Scott said. "I think she means Project Blastoff was a grown-up thing to do."

Mom nodded. "That's exactly what I mean. Going into space is something not many kids have done."

"Technically, it's something *no* kids have done . . . except Scott," Mark said.

"I rest my case," said Mom.

Sometimes each twin could tell what the other was thinking. Now they looked at each other and decided without a word that Scott should ask their mom the obvious question: "Uh, what's your point?"

"That you boys get yourselves into more than the usual number of tough situations," Mom said, "and I know from experience what a lousy feeling it is when somebody needs help and you don't know what to do. This class is going to give you the knowledge you need to be helpful. And I bet one day, sooner or later, that knowledge is going to come in handy."

Scott Kelly never mentioned it to anyone, but he had a mental filing system for grown-ups' comments. That little speech of his mom's he filed in the category: Stuff I Probably Should've Paid Attention To.

And the way things turned out, he was absolutely right.

Astrotwins: Project Blastoff
By Mark Kelly
Reading Group Guide

About the Book

Energetic twins Mark and Scott Kelly plan to study their dad's calculator by taking it apart. After a disastrous result, their consequence for destroying the calculator is a week at Grandpa's house, doing chores. While the boys are there, Grandpa suggests they direct their energy and curiosity to building something. He suggests a go-kart.

However, Mark and Scott like to think bigger than a simple go-kart. They decide to build a spacecraft and become the first kids in space. With the help of brainy Egg, whose real name is Jenny, and other kids they meet, the group begins building a rocket that can launch into space. Working together, they finally are ready for the big launch day. Can they actually pull off a successful launch and send the first kid into orbit?

Prereading Questions

Is there a limit to what kids can do? If so, where would that limit be? Support your answers with examples from your life or articles you've read about great things kids have done, discovered, or achieved.

What does it take to send someone into outer space to

orbit the Earth? What kinds of things would you need for a trip into space?

Discussion Questions

1. What gives you the first hint Scott and Mark are lively, curious boys?

2. When Mark and Scott first discussed who would go into space, Mark said, "Girls can't be astronauts." What do you think of this statement and how does it show the social situation in the decade when they lived?

3. What is the relationship between Mark and Scott as brothers and with their parents? Are their interactions in any way similar to or different from your family's?

4. Mark and Scott do many chores around the house and in the yard. Do you have chores? Are they similar to or different from the chores done by the twins?

5. The library played an important part as the kids learned what they needed for their project. How do you use the library? Is it in the same way that the group did? What has changed in libraries since the 1970s?

6. Is the setting an important part of the book? Explain your answer.

7. When the kids were working on the rockets, why did the adults keep saying, "Don't blow anything up!"

8. Do you see changes in Mark and Scott as their plan progresses? How do they change, if so?

9. Mark said that math is a universal language. What does that mean? Do you agree with the statement?

10. President John F. Kennedy challenged the nation to put a man on the moon. Reread President Kennedy's quote and discuss its meaning and significance. Follow up with Grandpa's quote, "The president's point was that sometimes you do the hard thing because doing hard things is good for you." Have you had something happen in your life where you chose to do the hard thing? What was it? How did you feel afterward?

11. Could the twins have managed to get into space without the others? How did working as a group benefit the project and what did each person bring to the project?

12. Was the contest to decide who went into space a good one? Was it fair? What kind of a contest could the kids have done instead?

13. How did Mark feel when he won the contest to be the astronaut? How did Scott feel?

14. How do you think Mark felt when he couldn't be the astronaut after his injury? What do you think were Scott's feelings?

15. What is the value of making a schedule and sticking to it? Are there disadvantages to having a schedule?

16. What do you think about the missions being named Project Blastoff? What about the name for the rocket, Crazy 8? Can you think of other names that would suit the projects as well?

17. Why did Mark and Scott spend so much time practicing their simulations? Did it help when it came time for launch and orbit? Explain why.

18. What effect did the cookie crumbs have on the mission? Was it a good idea to have sent them? Explain the forces that caused the problem with the crumbs.

19. Discuss the consequences of the space mission, both from the point of view of the adults involved and the Crazy 8 team's classmates. Were the consequences fair and appropriate? Why or why not?

20. What were the three biggest obstacles Mark and Scott encountered in planning their rocket launch?

21. Who of the group do you think is most likely to end up with a career in space? Who might end up an astronaut? Who would be suited to work in Mission Control?

22. Scott and Mark learned many things from their adventure. Discuss some of the lessons they learned.

23. Review the Author's Note in the back matter. Discuss the parts of the book that are real and the fictional parts. How do you think author Mark Kelly's life influenced this story?

Writing

1. Write a descriptive passage about Scott's feelings as he launched and circled Earth in the rocket. Include how he felt at various times during the trip and upon landing.

2. Read about the Apollo 1 disaster in 1967. Write to explain the event and relate it to Mark and Scott's concern about going into space.

3. Write a summary of the story and identify the main idea and theme in it.

4. Write a personal essay about the adventure in the voice of Scott, Mark, Egg, or Barry.

5. Write a letter to one of your friends and try to convince the friend to join you in a plan for an adventure requiring building something that might not be a good idea. Describe the adventure and device you'll be making and persuade them to work with you.

Setting
1. Find examples from the book that show the times the events in the book are taking place.

2. Compare where the Kelly family lives with Grandpa's home. What differences in the locations helped lead the boys to build a rocket to launch one of them into space?

3. Could the story have been set in a later decade and still be the same story? Why or why not?

Characters
1. Describe the kind of boys Scott and Mark are and give examples from the book to support your description.

2. How did Scott and Mark feel about meeting Jenny for the first time? Why do you think they felt this way?

3. Why did Scott and Mark decide to call Jenny "Egg?"

4. What part did Egg (Jenny), Barry, and Howard play in developing the rocket and what jobs did they perform?

Would Mark and Scott have been able to successfully launch without their help?

5. What can you infer about Barry's brother, Tommy? What happened to him in the Vietnam War? How did this affect Tommy?

6. Discuss the relationship Egg and Steve Peluso have with each other. Why do you think they are so competitive? Is there a class or sport in which you are competitive with another person?

7. How did the different personalities come together to work and complete the rocket and what were their disagreements about? Did each person bring something different to the group and what resulted from their differences?

8. Compare and contrast two characters from the book. Identify the characteristics that made them disagree or work well together.

9. How did an event in the story affect one of the characters? Tell how it did and what resulted from that particular event.

10. Which character would you like to get to know better? Explain why.

Plot

1. Use the NASA site and books or articles about John Glenn's first trip into space to read or research the historical event. Describe the similarities and differences of Mark's trip with Glenn's actual flight.

http://www.cleveland.com/friendship-7/index.ssf/2012/02/friendship_7_john_glenns_space.html

2. What part did Grandpa and Nando Perez play in helping the group build their project? Could they have completed the mission without their help? Give examples of how they added to the project and enabled the kids to succeed.

3. In what ways did Mr. Drizzle play a critical part in helping with the project? Give examples from the book that show what he did.

4. Why was it important to the kids to keep the project a secret? Give evidence from the book that supports your explanation.

5. Identify the theme of the book and explain how different parts of the plot contributed to its overall theme.

6. Compare and contrast the adventure Scott and Mark had with another adventure from literature. Identify the pattern of the two books and tell how they are alike and different from each other. Were the themes somewhat alike? If they were, tell how.

7. Read a nonfiction book about early space flight. Compare and contrast the two stories. Were there differences in the science portrayed in the two books? (See bibliography in the book's back matter.)

8. Could middle school students really build a successful rocket and launch someone into space? Explain your answer.

Point of View and Structure
1. The story is told in third person. Why do you think the author chose to tell the story this way rather than from Mark's or Scott's first person point of view? Would it have

made a difference if it had been told in first person?

2. The story structure follows the events in chronological order. Explain how each chapter contributed to the building of the story. What would be the difficulties in using an order that was not sequential in this book?

3. How did the first chapter indicate events that might take place later in the book? Use details to show how the boys' behavior could lead to future events that took place.

Vocabulary

1. Choose several of the science vocabulary words and explain how the context helped you understand the meaning of the words.

2. Use the glossary in the back matter of the book to select three to five words. Look up the words and learn more about the object or principle and the science behind them. Write to explain the selected words and give an example of how it applies or is used.

3. Find two or three examples of figurative language and explain their meaning.

4. Did any of the language in the book give clues to the setting and period of time when the story took place? Give examples.

Science

1. What are Newton's Three Laws of Motion? Explain them in your own words and give an example of each one.

2. List some examples of the protective devices the group

used to keep Scott safe while he was in the spacecraft. Why do you need protection when traveling in space?

3. Explain the fuel source they used. How did the author make this sound as if it were actually a real kind of fuel?

4. Explain the force of gravity and discuss the problems launching a spacecraft has in relation to gravity.

5. How did Scott describe what he saw while in orbit? Discuss the feelings he experienced on takeoff and re-entry and relate them to science terms from the glossary.

6. Look up and read about the different kinds of electromagnetic energy. What kinds of electromagnetic radiation would Scott have encountered in space?

Technology
1. What technology tools are available now that were not around at the time of the book's setting? What tools were used at the time and what changes have taken place in technology since the 1970s?

2. Look up early computers. Discover what BASIC is and compare the early computers to those used today.

3. What was their communication solution and what went wrong? How was it repaired?

Engineering
1. What did Scott, Mark, and the other kids need to include on their control panel? Refer to the book and list the items they incorporated that are necessary for a successful flight.

Look at this diagram and see if you can identify any of the control panel items.

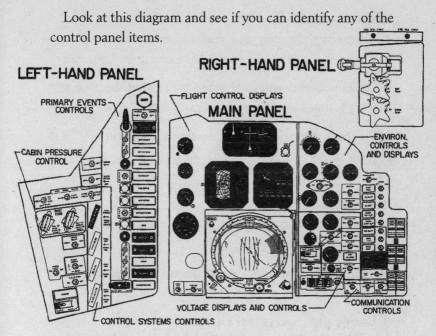

source: http://upload.wikimedia.org/wikipedia/commons/8/8b/Control_panels_mercury_atlas_6.png

2. Did the group behave like engineers in planning and building the project? How so?

3. Give examples of how the group overcame limitations in material available for building and fueling a rocket and space capsule.

4. What steps did the group take to learn what they needed to know in order to design their rocket?

5. Engineering is based on repeating and testing a process until the best design possible emerges. What flaw did the group have in their engineering of the spacecraft? Justify how they still could have succeeded, even without following a repeated testing series.

Mathematics

1. Research slide rules and read about them. Identify the parts and name them. Explain how to calculate using one.

2. Look up algebra and then review to see what the book says about algebra. Learn three terms associated with algebra.

3. Discuss the differences between mathematics and arithmetic.

Activities

1. Research Sir Isaac Newton. Make a presentation to show his biographical information.

2. Trace inventions from the 1970s up through today and create a technology time line to show the progress.

3. Design experiments that will show Newton's three laws of motion. Present them to another class or record them and give a class presentation.

4. Look up the books in your library that fall between 530 and 539 in the Dewey decimal system. What titles did you find? Would they have helped the group figure out the answers to their questions?

5. Listen to a recording of President Kennedy's speech about going to the moon. How does it differ from Grandpa's paraphrasing?

6. Investigate and research welding. What sorts of things are welded? What would you need to have and know before starting a welding project?

7. Plan a building project you might do with a group. Do

research to find out how to build your project. Set up dimensions and include the sizes and measures of each part of it. Inventory your materials, find out where to get what you don't have, and make a schedule. Carry out the plan if possible.

8. Create a chart of the different kinds of electromagnetic energy. Illustrate it and show examples of each kind of electromagnetic energy on the spectrum. Include wavelength diagrams.

9. Interview someone who used a slide rule during the 1950s—1970s. What were the advantages and disadvantages?

10. Read about waves. Make a diagram showing the vocabulary used to discuss waves and illustrate it with examples.

11. Research gyros. Report on them and how they work. Include their purpose and examples of practical use.

http://www.pilotfriend.com/training/flight_training/fxd_wing/gyro.htm

12. Look up Robert Goddard. What is he known for?

13. Role-play an interviewer talking to Mark and Scott after Scott's successful return to Earth. Write out the interview questions and the boys' answers. Present the interview or tape it and show it to the group.

Guide written in 2015 by Shirley Duke, a children's freelance writer.